Bound fo' Glory

Jean E. Holmes

Pacific Press Publishing Association
Boise, Idaho
Oshawa, Ontario, Canada

Edited by Glen Robinson
Designed by Dennis Ferree
Cover illustration by Mark Stutzman
Typeset in 10/12 New Century Schoolbook

Library of Congress Cataloging-in-Publication Data:

Holmes, Jean E., 1941-
    Bound fo' glory / by Jean E. Holmes.
        p.   cm. — (Weldon Oaks series ; pt. 5)
    ISBN 0-8163-1275-3 (pbk : alk. paper)
    1. South Carolina—History—Civil War, 1861 - 1865.
2. Afro-Americans—South   Carolina—Sea   Island—
History—19th century. 3. Plantation life—South Carolina—
Sea Island—History—19th century. 4. Sea Island—History.
I. Title. II. Series: Holmes, Jean E. 1941- Weldon Oaks
series ; pt. 5.
PS3558.035937B68 1996
813'.54—dc20   95-32386
                                                          CIP

96 97 98 99 00 • 5 4 3 2 1

Contents

Chapter 1: A Brick Outten Ol' Satan's Wall   7

Chapter 2: De Debt I Owe   21

Chapter 3: Follow Me Down ta de Jordan Stream   36

Chapter 4: Sweet Land of Liberty   46

Chapter 5: Out ob de Mucky Mire   53

Chapter 6: Fields of Endless Days   63

Chapter 7: Believer I Know   77

Chapter 8: On Sweet St. Helena Isle   88

Chapter 9: Goodbye, Brudder; Now God Bless You   100

Chapter 10: Uncle Billy's Bummers   107

Chapter 11: Do Remember Me   118

Chapter 12: Come Judgment Day   131

Chapter 13: At Home and Free!   144

Epilogue   155

Dedication

This book is dedicated
with my deepest love
to my daughter, Becky.

Chapter 1

A Brick Outten Ol' Satan's Wall

(December 1862)

Laura May sat in the parlor of Cousin Maude's home and listened to the sounds of the house. All was quiet. Mama was still napping in her bedroom. Cousin Maude was out in the yard feeding the last of her pathetically thin chickens. For a few precious moments, Laura May was alone. How she needed this time just to think, to mull over the new problem that now absorbed her every waking hour.

The afternoon had grown steadily colder. In all likelihood, there would be a frost before morning. This did not bode well for Laura May's plans. She must find a medium-size pair of man's boots, and quickly, for if the weather changed and the cold snap persisted, boots would be in short supply.

Poor Jonathan, she thought. *He'll have a dreadful time if the ground freezes.* She knew that his boots, the ones he had been captured in, were beyond redemption.

Actually, Corporal Jonathan Franklin was better off than most, for few of the Union prisoners in Camp Sorghum, which lay on the outskirts of Columbia, had anything at all to cover their torn and blistered feet. Dressed in rags and looking more like living skeletons than soldiers, the poor wretches huddled close to the ground in small, desperate packs or dug down into the dirt like burrowing animals.

Day after day she had watched their suffering. Scalded by a

merciless sun in the summer, exposed to the elements of wind and rain in the spring and fall, lying on the cold, bare ground throughout the winter—it was unconscionable that any human beings could be treated this way.

Oh, she had heard all the stories of how Confederate soldiers were being kept in Northern prisons. No doubt they were true, but it didn't make what happened here in Camp Sorghum right. She thought of Gilly and wept bitterly for him. Would he survive his imprisonment? If only she might have some word of him from Angel. But nothing had come through the lines for months, not even the smallest scrap of a message. Had any of her letters reached Coosaw? She had no way of knowing.

Her mind drifted back to Jonathan. It was odd how she felt about him. He was a Yankee, and, therefore, the enemy. She should feel nothing but contempt for him. But she couldn't, not after what he had done for her. That day in Columbia when she had been first attacked by the drunken sawyer, then almost trampled to death by a mob who were intent upon stoning the Union prisoners being marched through town—it had been a double nightmare. It was Jonathan who had saved her. Though in grave danger himself, he had reached out and pulled her to her feet, then sheltered her with his own body. Was that the act of an enemy? Hardly!

In the intervening months, Laura May had come to know Jonathan better. A visit to an old friend of her mother's had led to those first trips of mercy to Columbia's prisoner-of-war stockade. That's when she had met Jonathan again. How odd that it had worked out that way, almost as though it had been meant to happen.

She still went to see him, and the others, several times a week. Her meager offerings of food and clothing did little to assuage the terrible suffering of those men, but it was better than nothing. But now, Jonathan's steadily deteriorating condition alarmed her. She had to get him away from there somehow. If she didn't do it soon, he'd be dead.

Laura May had seen some of the bodies being carried out past the stockade's dead line. There was a long trench out there where they were dumped. A few more every day. Dirt thrown over them. The trench made a little longer. More bodies. More dirt. Day after day, the same horrifying cycle.

Jonathan had told her that he was often assigned to the burial brigade. Laura May thought long and hard about that. Perhaps that would be the best time for him to attempt an escape. But then, on one particularly bright day in early December, she had realized the futility of it. She was just leaving the stockade when a burial detail came out through the gate and headed for the trench. Stunned by the cadaverous bodies being dragged along by men who could barely stand erect themselves, she had found herself frozen in place.

Then suddenly, and without warning, two prisoners from the burial detail dropped their grizzly burden and took off for the woods. They never made it, not even as far as the trench. A salvo of rifle fire gunned them down. The guards left them lying where they'd fallen.

Laura May felt certain that one of those men was still alive, for she saw him try to move. But when the burial was completed, the guards ordered the remaining prisoners to lift up their fallen comrades and dump them into the trench. As the dirt was shoveled over them, Laura May felt herself grow faint with shock and disgust. How could anyone be so inhumane? she wondered.

No, she decided, Jonathan must never attempt such a thing! It was she who must find a way to get him out. But how? How?

The idea, when it came to her, was so simple that it fairly took her breath away. Why hadn't she thought of this before? Oh yes, it would still involve a terrible risk for Jonathan, but surely it was the only way. And others had made it. She had heard about the successful though infrequent escapes. And she had heard something else too. There was a lifeline, of sorts, much like the underground railroad. But instead of carrying escaped slaves to safety, this human chain of selfless Samaritans led escaped Yankee prisoners to the Union-held territories.

There were a legion of problems involved with her plan. First, she must find a way to distract the guards—something startling enough to give Jonathan time to make that first treacherous dash. She already had some ideas about that. It was just a matter of getting up enough courage to actually do what must be done.

Laura May had not been oblivious to the ogling eyes of the guards when she visited the stockade. Perhaps, by a little well-placed flirting, or even something that might be considered slightly scandalous, she could cause enough of a stir to give Jonathan the chance he needed. Yes, that was it. And for now, she need not work out the details; in this way, she would not have to agonize over the possibility of being dreadfully humiliated. The hardest part of her plan would be to make the proper contacts with those in the lifeline. One false move, and everything would be lost. She decided that her best hope lay in going back to the elderly black man who had taken her messages to Angel. He seemed trustworthy enough. But would he be willing to risk his life for such a dangerous cause?

Deciding to wait not a moment longer, Laura May went into the kitchen, opened the door of Cousin Maude's pantry, and took out a basket of eggs, which the old woman had been carefully hoarding. There'd be the very devil to pay when Maude found out that they were gone, but none of that mattered now.

She took the porch steps two at a time, then set off at a brisk trot. Heading for the road that led to the Negro shantytown down by the river, Laura May tried not to think too hard about what she was doing. Fear stalked her every footstep, for dusk was coming on, and the shantytown was no place for a lone white woman. A band of half-drunken soldiers hooted at her from a side alley. Ignoring them, she hurried on. She kept her head down and pressed the basket of eggs close to her breast. Fortunately, the tumbled-down dwelling she was heading for was on this side of the shantytown. She did not have too far to go.

She was panting with fear when she finally reached her destination. "Mister Cato?" she called as she knocked hesitantly on the door. Silence. Taking a deep breath, she called out louder.

"Mister Cato, are you in there?"

A shuffling sound came from behind the rough door. "What you want?" There was nothing friendly in either the voice or the question.

"I—I'd just like to talk to you for a moment, if I might. It—it's Laura May. Laura May Weldon. Do you remember me?"

The door opened a crack. She could see the glint of dark eyes, but there seemed to be no face behind them. "What you want?" came the belligerent voice once more.

"Is it Mister Cato I'm talking to?" she asked. "I—I can't see your face."

The door opened a bit wider. "What you doin' down he'e in shantytown, gal? Hain't you got no sense?"

Yes, it was the man she knew only as Cato. She reached out and handed him the precious basket of eggs but made no attempt to speak. Surprised, the old man looked down at the eggs, then back at Laura May's face. "Dis mus' be a ha'd t'ing you es gwanna axe ob me, bringin' all dem eggs like-a dat." He motioned her into the shack. "Et's a plum mi'acle you made et dis fa', gal, carryin' such val'able goods." His voice had softened slightly.

"Yes, that's true, Mister Cato. I do have something I need you to do. And—and I won't try to fool you, either; it's very dangerous." She pressed her trembling hands hard against her skirts.

"You kin set down effen you wants," Cato said. He pushed a rickety chair toward her. Sighing with relief, she slumped down into the chair. He was at least willing to hear her out. That was a good sign.

"You were so kind to me, Mister Cato, when I asked you to take those letters to my friend down in the Low Country. Do you remember that?"

"Um-hmm, I 'members you, all right, but I didn' take dem letters down ta de Low Coun'ry."

Laura May's heart nearly dropped into her stomach. He hadn't delivered the letters after all. No wonder she had heard nothing from Angel. Oh, what a fool she had been! She should have realized that it was too much to even hope for.

"Took 'em ta an ol' black 'oman I knows 'bought five miles down ribah," continued Cato. "An' she done took 'em ta anuder pusson what libes 'bout ten miles fudder on."

Laura May's head snapped up. "Then—then there's a chance that they got as far as Beaufort?"

"Bowfo't? I taught you wanted dem lettahs ta go ta Coosaw?" he answered with surprise.

"Yes. Yes, of course. But I hardly expected that—" She couldn't finish. There was a lump in her throat that was choking her.

"Dem lettahs went ta Coosaw," Cato said emphatically. "You t'inks I hain't gwanna earn mah pay!"

Laura May felt certain that she was about to cry. The lifeline! She had found it! Cato was a part of it. *Oh, God!* she cried to herself. *Thank You! Thank You!*

For the next half-hour, Laura May poured out her soul to the old black man. She told him of how she had first met Jonathan. She told him of the horrors of the prison camp, of the burial details, and of her hopes to help Jonathan escape. "You just can't imagine how inhumane that place is!" she cried. "Why, they treat them like animals—no—worse than animals."

Cato nodded his head and answered her quietly. "Yessum, Miss Laura May, I kin sho nuff 'magine what dat's like." Cato reached out and laid his wrinkled old hands on hers. "What you gwanna do, Miss Laura May? How you gwanna get dat boy past de so'diers?"

She dropped her eyes and began to study her hands. "I-I have sort of a plan. Perhaps it will work." Lifting her head, she looked straight into Cato's eyes. "But there's no need for you to worry about that. Just be somewhere nearby. Somewhere in the woods just north of the camp. If you can get to him in time—well—then I guess you would know what to do."

He shook his head and smiled. "Um-hmm," he said. "Don' you worry none. You jes get dat boy pas' de guards, an' ol' Cato will take care ob de rest."

He was so confident, so reassuring, that Laura May found her worries begin to melt away. "I'll do the best I can to pay you what this is really worth to me," she said.

Cato grinned at her. "What's a pusson's life wurt', Miss Laura? I hain't neba figu'd et out." Then, to her surprise, Cato did a very strange thing. Reaching into the basket, he took out just one egg. Placing it carefully on the splintered boards of his table, he turned around and handed the basket back to Laura May. "Dat's all I needs," he said gently. "I libes jes one day at a time, an' I hain't nebah in mah whole life ate mo' den one egg in a day."

Laura May did cry then. She broke down and wept. Cato let her get it all out. Wiping away the last of her tears, Laura May looked up at the old man with thankful eyes. What more could she say when he had already given her so much?

Cato personally escorted Laura May back to Cousin Maude's house. It was dark when they arrived, and Mama was frantic with worry. Maude watched Cato as he walked away into the darkness. She glanced down at the basket of eggs Laura May still clutched in her hands. "May I ask what this is all about?" she questioned.

Laura May raised her chin and looked straight into Cousin Maude's eyes. "I had something that needed to be done—and—and a debt to pay," she said hesitantly. "It would not be good for me to tell you more, Cousin Maude."

Maude raised one eyebrow, and with a look of speculation, tipped her head to one side. She reached out and took the basket of eggs from Laura May, then turned and walked toward the kitchen. Her back was very erect. "I was planning for us to have these eggs for supper," she said over her shoulder. "It's a good thing that there's still enough of them left to go around."

Just a week later, Laura May made her last trip to the prison stockade. Thankfully, the weather had warmed. She wore two petticoats under her skirts, each one of them, by careful selection, dangerously threadbare. Before leaving, she had kissed her mother goodbye.

"I shan't be too late, Mama, but if I'm not back by suppertime, don't wait for me."

Mama looked up at her with startled and frightened eyes. Cousin Maude gave her a darting glance, then became engrossed in the piece of handwork she was sewing on. "Your mother and I will be just fine," Maude said with a strange tightness to her voice. "But, child, do be careful. The city is full of dangers."

It was the first time that Maude had ever called Laura May "child." The endearment sounded strange on her lips, but there had been a definite sincerity to it. How much did Cousin Maude suspect? wondered Laura May. Had she suddenly become an ally?

When she arrived at the stockade, Laura May could see Jonathan standing by its northernmost fencing. There were two other prisoners with him. The little group seemed to be completely occupied with the construction of a small mud hut. But Laura May was certain that Jonathan had seen her. He had passed his hand twice across his forehead. It was their prearranged signal.

The guards were more or less evenly scattered around the camp's perimeter. Laura May had wished that they would be bunched closer together, but no matter. If her plan was going to work at all, she'd have their attention soon enough.

There were two other women already at the gate. Laura May knew them both and liked them immensely. She dreaded the thought of placing these good women in such danger, but then again, perhaps they might be useful. The more there were, the less likely any one of them would be suspected of abetting an escape.

Lifting her hand and waving to the women, she began to walk faster. How she hoped that no one had bent back into place that little bit of wire she had worked loose near the lower edge of the gate. But, no, there it was. Taking a deep breath, she purposely walked straight toward it.

Her plan worked even better than she had expected. The two women turned around to wait for her. Chattering lightly, though perhaps a bit too rapidly, Laura May stopped at the gate and reached out to place her hand on one of her friend's shoulders. "Oh dear, Sarah, please give me a hand for just a moment. I seem to have gotten something stuck in my shoe."

She leaned over and worked at the long laces of her left shoe, lost her balance, then grabbed once more for her friend's arm. "There, that's better. It must have been a pebble." She started to walk forward, apparently oblivious to the fact that her petticoats had somehow gotten caught on a ragged bit of wire.

There was a loud ripping sound. Laura May jerked herself around, but the sudden movement only made things worse. She lifted her skirt to survey the damage. Her outer petticoat, the weaker of the two, was torn from the hemline to well above her knees. The inner petticoat was also shredded, though not quite as badly.

There was a shrill whistle from the nearest of the guards. With her face going scarlet, Laura May quickly pressed down her skirt. But when she tried to move, her torn petticoats, which were still hopelessly snagged, only ripped all the more. Yanking at them frantically in order to extricate herself from the fence, and with the other women desperately trying to help her out of this embarrassing predicament, Laura May did not seem to notice the small knot of guards who were gathering nearby. There were more whistles and catcalls. Even some of the prisoners pricked up their interest and sidled over to the fence.

Then suddenly, from the north side of the stockade, there was a loud shout followed by the staccato sounds of gunfire. Through the crowd, Laura May could make out the forms of three prisoners racing for all they were worth across the slashed and opened land that surrounded the stockade. One of them fell, she couldn't tell who. Her heart was beating in her mouth. "Please, God, not Jonathan!" she whispered.

The woman standing closest to Laura May turned and gave her a sharp look. Then her eyes hooded over. She nodded knowingly, then turned away as though she had heard nothing.

There were more gunshots now, and the angry shouting of officers and guards. The two prisoners who had not fallen disappeared into the woods. A prison guard stood over the man who lay twisting in pain on the muddy ground. The angry guard lifted his rifle to his shoulder, aimed, and fired at point-blank range. Laura May hid her face in her hands. "Forgive me, Lord," she whispered. "Forgive me if I've made a terrible mess of this!"

Jonathan dashed headlong through the woods, with Louis close at his heels. They could hear the baying of bloodhounds somewhere to their right. If they didn't find a stream bed soon, they'd never get away.

Coming over a fern-covered rise, Jonathan felt his foot catch on an exposed root. He flailed out his arms, trying to grasp something—anything that would support him. It was too late. He could feel himself falling, tumbling head over heels down through brambles and briars until he finally came to rest in a deep, water-filled gully. No stream here. It was rainwater that had filled the depression, leaving it stagnant and fouled with rotting leaves.

"Jonathan!" Louis's voice was a hoarse whisper. "Where are you?"

"Down here. I think I've done something to my ankle." It was true. His ankle was throbbing and already beginning to swell.

"Oh, God help us!" cried Louis. "We'll never make it now."

"You go on, Lou. You can make it. Keep the sun to your right until dark. I'll see if I can slow them down."

Louis was working his way down the slippery embankment. "Don't be ridiculous, John. We go together, or we don't go at all."

"What about Harry?" asked Jonathan. "I don't think he even made it into the woods."

Louis was beside him now. " 'Fraid not. I looked back. They got him, all right, poor devil!"

"Maybe he's better off, Lou."

"Yeah, I was thinking that myself. Come on; there's no time to waste. Hang on to me, and I'll get you out of this sinkhole."

Pulling at Jonathan's arm, Lou got him to his feet, then half dragged him up the slippery sides of the gully. The baying of the hounds was much closer now. The sound carried through the woods like an oncoming storm.

They limped along, slower this time, making little headway. Then suddenly there was a noise directly ahead of them. The cracking of branches. A loud hooting sound, as though a disgruntled owl had been awakened from his afternoon slumbers.

"Hsst!" Lou stopped dead in his tracks. "What do you suppose that is?" There was terror in his eyes.

Jonathan had no time to answer. Suddenly, bursting through the woods came two enormous black men. Their kinky hair was disheveled and filled with broken bits of leaves and branches. Streaks of dirt and sweat ran down their faces in long, jagged lines. One man carried an ancient rifle with a barrel longer than his legs. The other held a machete, old and rusty, but still looking quite lethal.

Without so much as a grunt, the Negroes picked up the two escaped prisoners, slung them over their shoulders, and started off through the woods at a fast trot. Jonathan could not make a sound, for he was being bounced so sharply on the black man's shoulder that the wind was knocked clean out of him. He could hear Lou's angry protests, but there was nothing he could do to help his friend.

Somewhere along the way, Jonathan must have lost consciousness, for when he awoke, he was lying in a dimly lighted cabin. The smell of something wonderful wafted past his nose. His head felt fuzzy, and there was a loud ringing in his ears. Turning his head slightly, he made out the shadow of what looked like a large woman bending over a pot at a flickering fireplace.

The smell came again, rich and brothy. Jonathan felt ravenous, but his mouth was too dry to speak. Then the dark figure moved. Yes, it was a woman, very old and very black. Her eyes reflected the dancing flames as she moved her head rhythmically from side to side.

Then Jonathan realized that she was singing. Her words, virtually unintelligible, sounded completely foreign to his ears:

> Cum bul-le al-le
> Lilli-quam-be
> I wok om a mo-na

Cum bul-le al-le
Lilli quank.

"Please," Jonathan managed to get out of his mouth. "Water."

The woman turned suddenly as though startled. "Praise Gawd!" she shouted, throwing her hands up into the air. "You es alibe!"

She waddled rather than walked over to the low bed where Jonathan lay. "He'e, Yankee so'dier boy," she said gently. "Drink dis." Slipping her arm under his head, she lifted him as tenderly as a mother would lift a small child.

Cool water trickled into Jonathan's mouth. He half choked on it trying to get it down.

"Slow, Massa Yank. No needs fo' ta drowns youse'f." Then, clucking her tongue, she scrutinized him with troubled eyes. "Shame, shame, what dey done ta you. Mah ol' ruffle hen gets mo' beta scratch den what you mussa got!"

Jonathan took another long sip of the cooling liquid, then let his head sink back against the old woman's ample arm. She lay him down gently, waddled back to the fire, then returned with a wooden spoon and a steaming bowl of rich broth. Settling her frame down onto a dilapidated chair, she began to hand-feed Jonathan one small mouthful at a time. "Possum stew," she said by way of explanation. "Bes t'ing fo' ha'f-sta'ved Yankee so'diers."

He opened his mouth obediently and felt warmth and life begin to surge through his body. "Where am I?" he asked.

"Dat hain't impo'tant," answered the woman.

"Not in the prison stockade?" asked Jonathan, the fear coming back into his eyes.

"Lawd hab mussy, no!" answered the old woman. "You's in mah house, boy. An' you's gwanna stay he'e till you es fit ta trabble."

Jonathan raised himself up in alarm. "NO! I MUSTN'T—I-I CAN'T! THEY—THEY'LL CATCH ME!"

The old woman chuckled. "No, suh, Massa. Dis time we sho'

nuff hab done took a brick outten dat ol' Satan's wall!" She pushed him firmly back down onto the bed. "Hain't nosomebody gwanna ketch you. Not in mah house, dey hain't! Mah bo would rip 'em in two effen dey tried."

"Bo?" asked Jonathan. "Whose that?"

A glint of pride came into the old woman's eyes. "Dat's mah boy," she said. 'E's de one what pick you up in de woods an' brung you he'e."

"Oh," answered Jonathan. The memory of a gigantic, wild-looking black man came into his memory. "But—I—there were two of them, weren't there?"

The old woman chuckled deep in her throat. "You mean 'Possum John." She slapped her knee with glee. "Look like peas in a pod, don' dey? MIGHTY BIG PEAS!"

Jonathan found himself smiling. "Yes," he said. "Mighty big peas indeed!"

"Dey es cousins," answered the woman. "Bo'n widin de same week ob each uddah. Could pass fo' twins, dough, now hain't dat de trut'!"

Still smiling, Jonathan nodded. Then, with a start, he remembered Louis. "My friend?" he asked. "What happened to my friend?"

"You mean dat scruffy-lookin' sca'crow? He's jes' fine. Out wid de boys doin' some huntin'. Be back soon."

Jonathan felt his eyes growing heavy. All seemed to be well, though he had no idea where he was. Turning his head to one side, he soon fell fast asleep.

It was daybreak when he opened his eyes again. Louis was standing over him with a worried look tracing long lines across his forehead. "John!" Louis knelt down by the bed and placed his hands on Jonathan's chest. "I thought for certain we were going to lose you. You've been asleep for days."

"Where are we, Lou?"

"Search me, John. Someplace in South Carolina, I guess. But east of Columbia. The land is much flatter here and desolate as an old maid's trousseau. Guess we're just plain lucky, though. If those two bucks hadn't come across us, we'd be crow meat by now."

"It wasn't just luck," said Jonathan matter-of-factly. "I didn't want to tell you this in case we didn't make it, but Laura May—that's the young woman who's been coming to the stockade with food—she arranged all of this."

"Whew!" Lou let out a loud whistle. "It sure is nice to have friends in high places!"

"Can you believe it?" Jonathan himself sounded incredulous. "What a gem that girl is! If ever a man got repaid for a simple act of kindness, it was me."

"So who is she, John? I mean, really."

"A Southerner. A refugee from a place down on the coast called Beaufort. She and her mother had to come up to Columbia when a Union armada took over the Sea Islands where she lived."

"Well, bless my soul! Beaufort, you say? That's just where we're heading. That fellow, Possum John, said he was going to take us about five more miles down river and hand us over to someone else. It's sort of like a rescue line. One person takes you for eight or nine miles; then he passes you over to someone else, who takes you a few more miles, and so forth. Negroes, all of them. Most of them slaves. Trying to help Yankee soldiers get back to their own lines. They'd be lynched or worse if they ever got caught."

"Then we'd best not stay here much longer," Jonathan said. "I don't want anything to happen to these good people."

He turned over onto his side and sighed. Louis looked down at him and smiled. "What are you thinking about, my good man?"

"I'm thinking of a girl who can't seem to keep her petticoats in one piece. I'm wondering if I'll ever in this world get to see her again."

Chapter 2

De Debt I Owe

(November 1862)

Angel was frightened. Never before had she come this far into the thick woods with only an hour or two of daylight to spare. She considered herself a daring person, but now her boldness seemed to have deserted her. She did not like traveling alone in a night-shrouded forest. The look of the sky and the heaviness in the air left her feeling apprehensive. Danger seemed to lurk in every shadow and behind every bush.

Pressing her body tightly against the coarse fur and bristly hairs of Gabriel's neck, Angel shuddered. The little marsh tacky was as sure-footed as any animal of the woods, but she did not trust her own ability to remain mounted on such a rough and slippery trail. It had been raining for days. The sky was the same murky color as the puddles of water that covered large areas of the trail. Laden with moisture, tree branches and garlands of Spanish moss brushed against the ground, making her journey all the more difficult.

Somewhere to her right, she heard the cry of an owl. Deceived by the leaden skies, the night creatures were astir and beginning to hunt. Their eery sounds brought all of the old tales back to Angel. Witches and hags, plat eyes and spirits—evil things that haunted the darkest hours of the night.

Not that she accepted such tales. "How silly ob me!" she said, her words echoing in her ears. "Dey es jes' superstitious tales."

The words were convincing, but still she couldn't keep the tremor from her voice.

Perhaps the events of the day brought Angel these feelings of edginess. She had left her own comfortable cabin early this morning to go to the far end of the island. There was a young woman in labor there with her first child. Angel had promised to assist with the delivery. The birth had not been difficult, but as the infant slid from its mother's womb, a gasp went up from the old grandmother who stood nearby. "Lawd hab mussy!" she'd said with her hands against her mouth. "Dere's a caul 'pon she face!"

Indeed, it was true. The infant had been born with the birth membrane still covering her tiny face. Nonplussed, Angel carefully removed it, but the grandmother was insistent "dat de propa t'ings mus' be done."

Taking the detached caul to the hearth, the old woman carefully parched it over a warm brick until it was dry. Then, using a wooden pestle, she ground the remains into a soft powder. After brewing a weak tea, she added to it a few pinches of the powdered caul. Finally, using the tip of her little finger, the old woman forced a bit of the concoction into the baby's tiny mouth. Satisfied, the grandmother sat back and smiled. "Now den," she said, "I reckon dat'll keep de ebil sp'rits from giben she de conbulsions."

It was a belief as ancient as the continent of Africa and as persistent as the arts of root workers or the spells of conjure doctors. A baby born with a caul on its face would be haunted by visions. Possessing such "second sight," or the ability to see the spirits of the deceased, was not considered entirely bad, for as long as the proper precautions were taken at birth, the ghostly beings would have no power to harm the child.

Angel had seen this rite performed many times, but she still felt uneasy about it. She had personally rejected the idea of the spirits of the dead, evil or otherwise, communicating with the living. But to believers, the superstitions could do strange and sometimes frightening things. A strong and healthy man might sicken and die simply because he *believed* that he had been conjured or that the evil eye had been put upon him. Black magic and voodoo were especially dangerous, for they were often associated with devil worship.

Thus, while she was not a believer in the superstitions, Angel felt quite certain that evil forces did exist and were ever ready to invade the minds of the unwary. She had done her best to teach this to the patients she nursed. But all too often, it was a losing battle. The beliefs persisted.

So it was that on this, of all days, the hooting of the owl had been especially unwelcome to Angel. It was one of the worst of the signs. An owl hooting close by in the early evening meant that someone was going to die. And believer or not, the very thought was enough to send shivers up her spine.

Four days of heavy rains had kept Angel from going into the deep woods of Coosaw. This was bad, for she had a mission in the woods—a mission that could make the difference between life or death to someone very close to her. In the leather pack strapped across Gabriel's back, Angel carried food and medicines. The people of the island were used to seeing her traveling the back trails with her pack, but on this particular trip, it was essential that no one know of her exact destination. It was for this reason that she had waited until late in the day to make the journey.

But now the sodden sky was forcing the night to fall early, and the woods were filled with sounds. Unwelcome ones. Frightening ones. Even Gabriel seemed to quiver as he walked. Angel pressed herself close to his warm body and prayed for one last watery shaft of sunlight. But none came.

Finally, in the gloom ahead of her, she saw the dark outlines of ruined walls. She raised herself slightly and let out a quiet, birdlike call. It was answered almost immediately. Angel sat erect. Prodding Gabriel with her bare heels, she called again, but this time she used a name.

"Gilly? Gilly, es you dere?"

A silent, spectral figure moved amongst the shadows. A hand was raised, but there was no answering call.

Angel slid from Gabriel's back. It was hard for her to walk, for she had been crippled from birth with clubbed feet that twisted over at a grotesque angle. She usually wore her skirts long to hide her deformed feet. But for traveling through the woods with its grasping vines and low-hanging branches, she chose to wear only a shift cut well above the calves of her legs.

Reaching up for her crutches, which she had carefully strapped beneath her pack, she placed them under her arms, then sidled awkwardly forward. "Gilly?" she said again, this time more insistently.

The figure moved from the shadows and came toward her. He nodded his head. "It's been days," he said, his voice flat and lifeless.

Angel reached out her hand and touched the young man's ragged sleeve. "I sho' am sorry, Massa Gilly, but de rains—" She ended her sentence before she was through with it, for he was waving her off as though he understood but chose not to hear more.

Walking toward the marsh tacky with slow, stumbling steps, Gilly undid the pack and slung it over his shoulder. Saying nothing, he turned, motioned for Angel to enter the tumbled-down building, then silently followed her.

Again, Angel felt a tremor move through her. Gilly was slipping away. Not physically so much, but mentally. He did not have the temperament to live like a hermit, closed away from the world of humans. Depression seemed to have settled over him like a mask that allowed for no facial expressions. This, too, frightened Angel. It frightened her more than the dark woods or the sounds of the night.

Gilly was slipping away, and for the time being, there was nothing she could do about it. The island was crawling with Yankee soldiers. It was only the good Lord's mercy that had kept them away from these woods, but how long would that last? Indeed, Angel was beginning to wonder if it wouldn't actually be more merciful to allow Gilly to be recaptured. If he went back to the prison stockade, he'd at least have contact with his own people.

The young black girl meant well, for she had little knowledge of the conditions in the stockade on Hilton Head where Gilly had been imprisoned. She had seen the results of his confinement, but only well after the fact. Thus, she had attributed Gilly's poor health, not only to scant food, but also to a lack of proper wound healing. Gilly had been badly injured during the battle of Port Royal Sound.

Gullah Jim, the old plantation fisherman who had rescued Gilly following the younger man's escape, had told Angel nothing of the starvation and deplorable conditions that the prisoners of war endured in the Hilton Head stockade. Indeed, there had been no time for Jim to tell anyone. Tragically, he had been killed in the effort to bring Gilly back to Coosaw.

Oh, thought Angel as she watched Gilly wolf down the food she had brought him, *if only Gullah Jim be still alibe*! No one had expected the old man to be shot down like that. Jim had been like an anchor in their lives—always there when needed, always ready to support and protect. Every time she turned around, Angel felt certain that she would see him again.

How much of Gilly's depression was caused by the old fisherman's death, Angel could not be certain, but she felt sure it played a part. He had loved the old man dearly and must surely be suffering some amount of guilt over his loss.

Despite having traveled through a gloomy woodland, Angel found that her eyes did not easily adjust to the oppressive darkness within the derelict walls of the old Praise House. And this, too, was a reason for Gilly's depression. No one could possibly live here day after day and night after night without being terribly altered by it.

Neither had the constant dampness helped. Of late, Gilly had developed a persistent cough. He tried to suppress it when Angel was present, but he could never completely hide it from her. In her pack she carried medicines, which she hoped would make him better. But getting away from this dank place and into bright sunshine was what was really needed. And no amount of medicine would cure Gilly until that happened.

It wasn't likely to happen soon, though. The war was dragging on with no end in sight. Young men were fighting and dying by the thousands. Refugees streamed away from one battle zone, only to be caught up in another. Even Zach, Angel's one true love, had been sucked up by the insanity of the war.

Zach. The very thought of him made Angel's heart grow lighter. If only he were here to help her. He was no Gullah Jim, but he'd know what to do about Gilly. Zach and Gilly were the closest of friends.

Sold on the Charleston auction block at the tender age of six, Zach had been brought to Weldon Oaks to serve as the young master's personal servant. Quick-witted and desperate for friendship, Zach had soon altered his status in Gilly's eyes. And before the two of them were anywhere near their teens, they had become inseparable companions. Well, almost inseparable.

Gilly had gone off to Annapolis in the fall of 1860, leaving Zach behind to ponder the sudden change in their relationship. It had been a bitter moment for the black boy. For with Gilly's going, Zach's standing in the Weldon household had immediately dropped, and with it went much of his hard-earned self-confidence.

Misunderstandings, though never far from the surface, also began to fester between Angel and Zach after Gilly's departure. Angel had loved Zach since she was a child, though, sadly, he had been oblivious to the fact. But as the years matured Angel, Zach started to take notice of her. Finally, just weeks ago, he had declared his intentions to marry her. But poor Zach, he could never be free of the demands that he placed upon himself. It was as though he were constantly trying to prove something. Angel didn't know what it was. She doubted that Zach did either.

In the autumn of 1861, with the war raging in the tidewater states, a Union armada had invaded Port Royal Sound and taken firm control of the islands surrounding it. The area's enslaved people had been immediately set free. Jubilation Day had come early for them, far earlier than it would for the Africans still shackled by slavery throughout the rest of the South.

Momentous things began to happen on the South Carolina Sea Islands because of this Union victory. Missionaries came—

teachers and preachers, doctors and nurses, administrators and organizers—men and women of great vision and much fortitude. Schools were started for the freedmen, for adults as well as children, sweeping away in mere weeks what blind prejudice and oppressive laws had taken years to construct. Cultivated land once owned by the powerful few was turned over, two or three acres at a time, to the men who had once worked it as slaves. Cornfields and garden plots flourished where only cotton had grown.

Angel found the changes both exhilarating and challenging. Slavery had not been quite the same burden for her as it had been for others, for she'd been one of the favored. When her mother had died after giving her birth, Angel was taken to the Big House to live with her grandmother, who served as the nursemaid for the planter's children. Maum Beezie held sway in that house as few black women could ever hope to do. Her word was law. Even Master Weldon deferred to her wishes. Of course, she had never overstepped her bounds, but still she had had the power.

That power had been Angel's protective shield throughout most of her childhood. And along with Maum Beezie's authority, there had been a sisterly sort of friendship between Angel and Laura May, the master's young daughter. Laura May was gone now, driven away, both she and her mother, by the victorious Union forces. But Angel still longed for the girl who had been brave enough, even as a young child, to defy the unjust laws and biased conventions of the day.

Born within a month of each other, Angel and Laura May had been as inseparable as Gilly and Zach, if not more so. Showing no real favoritism, Gilly had been protective and brotherly with both of the girls. Thus, with her own indomitable will and so much love surrounding her, Angel had seldom been hampered by her physical disability. She saw this as a debt owed, one that she could not easily set aside, even now, with fear chasing her every footstep. Gilly needed her, so she had come. It was just that simple. She would do the same, if she could, for Laura May.

Gilly finished his meal, then without speaking, went to stand in the doorway. He looked terribly thin. His hair had grown long and scraggly. An unkept beard elongated his face but did nothing to fill in the hollows of his cheeks. His shoulders were perpetually slumped, his hands trembled even when at rest, and his ragged clothes hung on his tall frame like loose gunny-sacks.

Angel stared at his back, uncertain of what she might do to lift his spirits. "Big doin's soon," she said lightly, though some-what tentatively. "Lots ob peoples es comin' from all ober de place—St. Helena Island, Lady's Island, eben Edisto."

Gilly's only reply was an unintelligible grunt.

"Dem preacher mens from de no'th es gwanna be he'e ta talks ta de so'diers. Hear tell dat eben Deacon Brown from St. Hel-ena es comin', an'—an' mayhap eben Sam'l." She had named Samuel only as a casual last, for she wasn't sure how Gilly would react to the idea of Coosaw's former Praise House Watch-man coming back.

Samuel had befriended Gilly and Zach when they were quite young. Even then, in his early twenties, Samuel had been an ox of a man. And his bravery matched his size. It was Gilly's own father who had appointed Samuel as the Praise House Watchman, a position that gave him considerable leadership, both spiritual and otherwise, within the plantation's slave com-munity.

Though completely unlettered, Samuel had done an admi-rable job as the spiritual leader. Unfortunately, his longings for freedom were not to be contained by responsibilities and titles. Samuel had been determined to make good his escape from Coosaw, not just to save himself, but ultimately to free others also.

Here, too, was a bone of contention, for Zach had been al-most undone when Samuel made his escape. Left without the mature influence of the man he idolized, Zach's spirit seemed wounded beyond repair. It was Angel, as usual, who had had to pull him through.

Then Samuel started making periodic contact with the former

members of his flock. He had become a part of the secret Underground Railroad, joining Harriet Tubman as a champion of mass escape and organized rebellion. Master Weldon had denounced him as a villain worthy of death, but to Zach, the hero image had only grown more lustrous.

Nowadays the one-time Praise House Watchman was known to his people as Reb'nd Sam'l. It was an appropriate title. Though he had acquired only a smattering of book learning, Samuel could deliver a sermon to stir the soul of the most hardened reprobate. Angel had heard him preach just three weeks ago. Then and there, she'd been converted.

How she longed to tell Gilly of this! She wanted to tell him about the baptism that was to take place in just a few days' time. She wanted to tell about the decision that she had made to go down into the sin-cleansing waters with the other baptismal candidates. But upon careful reflection, Angel doubted that Gilly would understand. He had become cynical and embittered by the loss of his home and family and by the hard circumstances of his imprisonment. Gullah Jim was gone. His best friend Zach had, in a sense, deserted him. And on the few occasions when Angel had talked of Samuel, Gilly's reaction had been to turn sullenly away. It was as though the relationships of his past no longer mattered. He had become cold, indifferent, and distant.

But this time when Angel mentioned Samuel, Gilly's reaction surprised her. He turned to face her, his eyes riveting into hers. "Why's he coming?" he asked suddenly.

"Wh-why's who comin'?" Not suspecting such a question, Angel was left off balance.

"Samuel, of course. You said Samuel was coming to Coosaw."

Angel gave him a straightforward answer. "Ta preach ta de colo'd folks, ob course."

"And?"

"What you mean, Gilly?"

"And what else? He's coming for more than just preaching, isn't he?" Gilly's eyes were cold and guarded.

"I—uh, well, I reckon' so. 'E's comin' fo' ta baptize too. Gwanna be a pow'ful big baptism down by de ribah."

"Ah," answered Gilly. "Then he's got himself quite a following, does he?"

Angel looked up quizzically. Something strange was stirring
in this young man, a subtle spark of fire that seemed to have
little to do with either friendship or things spiritual.

Walking over to the bench, Gilly sat down beside her. Dwin-
dling light filtered through the lush vegetation beyond the broken roof and the ruined walls, turning his face to the color of
weathered copper. But his eyes had come alive, and his hands,
though trembling, felt hot on her forearms.

"And what of Zach?" he asked, holding her arms in a tight,
almost painful grasp. "Where is he now?"

Again, Angel felt a tremor of fear. She answered quietly, "Wid
de Union A'my ober at Camp Saxton. Dey all's been trainin'
mighty hard lately, 'cause de talk es dat dey's goin' down souf
ta some ribah—" She cut her sentence short, fearful that she'd
already said too much.

Gilly's face changed. "Ah-ha!" he hissed. "So, he's joined
Colonel Higginson's black regiment after all. I suspected as
much."

Angel's mouth fell open. She swallowed hard, then nodded.
Had she told Gilly about Colonel Higginson and the newly
formed black regiment? Odd, she couldn't remember having
done so, but then she must have. How else would he know about
such a thing? A small warning light began to flash in the back
of her mind. She looked at Gilly closely now, seeing the changes
in his face and the strange, burning light in his eyes. And suddenly she felt as though she were seeing a stranger. The feeling was both eerie and frightening.

Still, Gilly wasn't finished with her. "So tell me, will the entire regiment be going into Georgia, or just a few companies?"
Angel shrugged her shoulders and shook her head. The conversation, if that's what this was, had taken an uncomfortable turn.

Gilly stood up and walked slowly toward the doorway. He
was muttering to himself, but she could hear enough of his
words to understand what he was saying. "The Saint Mary's

River? No, nothing there to speak of. Then perhaps the Saint John's. But why? Jacksonville? Possibly. Easy pickings. Then again, maybe not. Certainly they'd meet plenty of resistance."

He paced back and forth nervously, still mumbling to himself. "Raw recruits—scatter with the first shot—the Saint Mary's, then. Yes—closest—might meet a few patrols, though."

Gilly turned and looked back at her speculatively. He scratched at the stubble on his chin but said nothing. Angel could see that his mind was working over some difficult problem. Could he be right? she wondered. If Colonel Higginson did plan to take his new regiment south, and thence up either the Saint Mary's or the Saint John's, would there be rebel patrols waiting for them? She shuddered to think what might happen.

Then Gilly's hooded eyes came alive again. He held his mouth in a straight line and asked, "What about weapons, Angel? Negro soldiers have never been allowed to carry them in the past."

Angel looked at him in confusion. "Wha-what you mean, Gilly?"

"Angel, is the federal government actually arming its Negro troops? This regiment—it's experimental—something entirely new. There's got to be lots of opposition to it."

Angel slid backward on the bench as though to hide herself in the shadows. "Don' know 'bout dat, Massa Gilly. Zach, 'e hain't neber done tol' me 'bout such t'ings." Her answer was truthful, for she and Zach always avoided this particular subject. Zach knew how apprehensive she was about his army career.

"Hmm." Gilly seemed genuinely worried. "So—" He hesitated, then turned away as he continued to speak, but she could hear the tension in his voice. "I take it that you haven't been over to Camp Saxton."

"N-no, Massa Gilly. I hain't neber ben ta Camp Saxton. Zach, 'e won' 'llow et." And that, too, was the truth. Zach insisted that Angel stay well away from the black army camp. He said that he was concerned for her reputation, considering what most people thought of camp followers, but Angel often wondered if there might not be more to it than that.

Not satisfied with her reply, Gilly continued to press her. "Angel, surely Zach must have told you something. How long will they be gone? How many are going? It's just not like him to leave you in the dark about such things."

"No, Massa Gilly. 'E hain't neber said." Gilly was wrong. Zach never talked to her about the army.

"And Samuel? Where does Samuel figure into all of this?"

Angel's fear began to turn into frustration. She didn't know what Gilly was getting at, but he had no right to question her so vehemently! Was it that he distrusted her relationship with Samuel, or was something else bothering him? "Hain't I already done told you, Massa Gilly? Sam'l, 'e's gwanna be preachin' an' baptizin'. Anysomehow, what fo' you so riled up 'bout? How come et matter what Zach an' Sam'l es doin'?"

The warning light in her head was turning into an idea that was far more appalling than the possibility of Gilly's mistrusting her relationship with Samuel. Was it possible? No, surely not! But then again—maybe so. Could Gilly be a spy? Given the kinds of questions he was asking, it did seem plausible.

For one thing, there was something odd about Gilly's continued presence on Coosaw. Yes, she knew that Gullah Jim had brought him here to rebuild his strength, but given the dangers involved, why did he continue to stay on?

Gilly came back and sat down beside Angel. Looking into her face, he seemed to sense the nature of her fears. "Oh, Angel," he said, "I'm sorry! I—I don't know why I've been going on like this." Dropping his face into his hands, he let out a low sob. "You don't deserve to be treated like this, Angel. You've been good to me—better than I deserved. Jim's death—it—it really rattled me! What would I have ever done if it weren't for you and Maum Beezie?"

Lifting his face from his hands, Gilly reached out for Angel's arms. "They mustn't find me, Angel. They mustn't! I swear, I won't ever go back to that stockade—not willingly. No, I'd rather die first!"

Angel touched his face gently. "I—I wisht I could tell you mo' 'bout Zach an' Sam'l," she said quietly, "but—well—effen I do, et might could cause all kinds ob bad trouble. You unduhstan' what I'm sayin', Gilly?"

Gilly nodded.

"Lookee he'e." Angel's face brightened with a new thought. "Don' you worry none 'bout Zach. 'E es gwanna be fine. Why, I reckon dat ol' Zach es big 'nuff ta take care ob 'eself by now. An' Sam'l too. Sam'l's a good man, Gilly. A man ob God, and dat's de trut'. 'E hain't got de time fo' no shenanigans, not when 'e's got de wu'k ob de Lawd ta do!"

Gilly smiled wanly and shook his head. "Perhaps you're right—about Samuel, anyway. But Zach, huh, I just don't know about him. He's changed from when we were kids together. I thought that he'd learn to know when he was well off, but it doesn't seem to have happened."

Gilly grasped Angel's arms with such firmness now that she almost winced. "Doesn't he know what a treasure he's got in you, Angel? I don't think so. No, I just don't think so." He shook his head angrily. "I'll tell you this; I'd really like to knock some sense into that thick head of his!"

Pulling gently away, Angel decided it was time to change the subject. "Gilly," she said, her face brightening again. "Did I eber tell you dat I got a letter from Laura May?"

Gilly's head jerked up. "A letter from Laura May? No. No, you didn't."

"Well, I hab. Got de letter jes de uddah day." It was partially a lie. Weeks had passed since she had received the letter. Gilly already knew that his mother and sister were in Columbia, but Angel had been hesitant to tell him of Laura May's latest news. Given his odd mood swings and his deep depression, she wasn't exactly sure how he'd take it.

"Well, then, what did she say?" Gilly asked impatiently. "I don't understand why you didn't bring it along so I could read it for myself. You know how anxious I am for her safety!"

Angel just shrugged and tried her best to look noncommittal. "Most ob what she say, you already know, Massa Gilly. Laura May an' yo mama, dey's managin'. Still libin' wid Cousin Maud. Doin' piece wu'k an' such ta keep food on de table."

"But what else? What else does she say, Angel?" Gilly prodded, intuitively knowing that there was more.

Trying to buy some time so she could think out her answer, Angel ran her finger slowly along a splinter of damp wood that stuck out along the edge of the bench. "Well, now—" She hesitated, keeping her head down and her eyes averted from his. "Et says sumpin' 'bout dis po' Yankee so'dier what Laura May's been he'pin'. Seems dis so'dier got 'ese'f captured, jes' like you done, Gilly. An'—an' 'e's in dis ter'ble prison place." She looked up at him then, her eyes pleading for understanding. "Like dat bad stockade you was in down on Hilty Head."

Gilly's mouth dropped open. "A prisoner? A Yankee prisoner? But—but I don't understand. Why would Laura May be helping a Yankee? Haven't she and Mama had enough trouble?"

Angel dropped her eyes into her lap again. "Well, suh," she mumbled, "I—I 'spect et's 'cause she might be sweet on him, Massa Gilly."

"WHAT!" Gilly's voice became shrill and incredulous. "What are you talking about, Angel? How do you know such a thing? Is that what she actually said in her letter?"

Going back to the splinter of wood, this time trying to work it loose, Angel hesitated before answering. "No, not en jes' dem words."

"Then what could possibly lead you to think that she's sweet on some fool Yankee?"

Angel lifted her head and looked defiantly into Gilly's eyes. " 'Cause I kin read atween de lines," she said. " 'Cause dere hain't nobody—not eben you, not eben yo mama—what knows Laura May like I do, Massa Gilly. She's sweet on dis Yankee, I knows dat fo' certain. An' what's mo', Gawd he'p she, I t'ink she's gwanna try sp'rit him away from dat place!"

Pulling away from her, Gilly stood up with a start. His face was as dark as the clouds. "You're crazy, Angel. Crazy! Why, Laura May would never try such a foolish thing. She's got more sense than that. Why—why, it would be far too treacherous." He swung around on her. "And treasonous to boot!"

The silence between them lasted for some time. Gilly's face

began to change. The hardness went from it, and in its place, there was something more akin to shame.

"Um-hmm," answered Angel finally, her eyes still on her hands. "Some folks might call et treason. Dat's de trut'." She lifted her head slowly and looked straight into Gilly's eyes. "An' et might could go pow'ful bad fo' Laura May effen somebody went ta doin' too much talkin' 'bout et."

It was Gilly's turn to drop his head. "Yes, I—I see what you mean." His words were barely audible. "I do see what you mean, Angel!"

Chapter 3

Follow Me Down ta de Jordan Stream

(December 1862)

Staying close to the ground, slithering on his belly at times in order not to be seen, Gilly inched closer to the creek bed and the tall marsh grasses that surrounded it. In the distance he could see a long, double line of Negroes winding their way slowly toward the bank of the nearby Coosaw River. The men were at the front, with Samuel, their preacher, in the lead. Samuel stood well above the others, his dark head erect, his stately stride filled with authority. He was majestic to look at and every bit the leader.

Gilly found it hard to pull his eyes away from Samuel, for he had always been fascinated by the man. But finally, purposefully turning his face toward the creek, he made himself search along its banks. He must be certain that his hiding place was secure.

The creek's waters, deep and winter dark, were growing restless. The tide was about to change. Even as he watched, Gilly could see an almost imperceptible shift. Then, as though an earthen dam were gradually giving way, the waters began to move. The flow was sluggish at first, but gradually, picking up speed, the waters began to surge outward. Gilly had seen this a thousand times: the tidal current, relentless, sucking from below, a brisk wind skating across the surface.

Watching the change and knowing what was about to happen at the edge of the river, he found himself shuddering. Was

Samuel a fool? Why was he holding a baptismal ceremony in such treacherous waters? Perhaps he saw himself as some modern-day prophet who could stop the course of the moon and alter the shifting tides. There was no telling what errant thoughts might be running through his mind. Gilly was certain that Samuel had become a fanatic.

His mistrust of this man whom he had once called friend was growing acute. Gilly's greatest fear was that Samuel would in some way, inadvertently or otherwise, bring harm to Angel. If that should happen—if there was even the first sign of it—Gilly was determined to see to it that Samuel paid dearly.

Hunkering close to the tall marsh grasses, Gilly waited for the slow-moving procession to draw closer. An old memory began to nibble at the inner fringes of his mind. How many years had passed since he and Zach had slithered along the ground like this, watching another such gathering of the Gullah people? Not a baptism then, but a religious ceremony nevertheless.

Ah yes, the Shout. It had been held in the deep woods of Coosaw very late at night. And the people had come, though in those days such congregating was strictly forbidden. They had sung much as they were singing now; the old, sweet spirituals that moved and swayed them like the steady sweep of a hoe biting deep into a dusty patch of ground.

Now here they were again, thought Gilly, his father's former slaves. So much had changed since those early days. The master was dead, and with him had gone the practice of slavery—at least on these islands. Gilly felt certain that this war would never come to a proper end until the rest of the South buckled under the pressure and did away with the cruel institution. He hated the very concept of slavery and wanted no part of it. His father's death had come as a terrible shock to him, but Gilly was glad that he would not have to deal with the headaches of owning cotton land and the slave labor it took to work it.

Angel had told Gilly of the latest talk. There was much speculation about turning a portion of the plantation lands over to the freedmen to do with as they chose. Gilly knew these people well. He knew that many would simply continue doing what they had done for generations—grow cotton. But now it would be different, for the profit would be theirs, not the master's. And by having a few acres that they could actually call their own, they'd be better able to feed their families. Surely it wouldn't take much land to plant a dozen rows of corn, a little okra, some collard greens, and a few bushes of field peas. Between all of that, they could put in their sweet potato and watermelon vines. Either way, it wouldn't matter much to him. The land wasn't his, never had been, for that matter. He was not cut out to be a planter and had no interest in farming.

The baptismal procession was drawing closer now. Gilly could hear the sounds of individual voices, for the air was clear and growing steadily colder. And the water? Surely it must be frigid, he thought.

Go back, Samuel. Take them all back and wait for a warmer day. Or better yet, dip your own hands in that cold water and sprinkle it over their heads. Why this way, this full immersion? Surely the God you serve won't mind so terribly much if, just this once, you bend the practice a bit!

> If-a you don' belieb Ah been redeem',
> Gawd's gwanna trouble de watuh.
> Follow me down ta dat Jordan stream.
> Gawd's gwanna trouble de watuh.

The people were singing, their voices blending in unison, their bodies swaying from side to side with a hypnotic rhythm. Still closer they came. Now Samuel's voice could be plainly heard above the rest.

> Who's dat yonduh dressed in white?
> Gawd's gwanna trouble de watuh.
> Must be de chillun ob de Israelite.
> Gawd's gwanna trouble de watuh.

Then he saw Angel walking submissively behind with the other women. How could he miss that awkward, stumbling gait?

It was odd, though, for despite her blundering feet, she carried her body with an unmistakable air of dignity. Like the other female candidates, she was dressed all in white. A white headpiece was wrapped turbanlike around her dark hair. Her long white robe swept erratically across the mud flats and marsh grasses like some low-flying egret hampered by an injured wing.

Don't do it, Angel, not today. The water's too cold. Think of yourself for just this once. Think of what it would do to Maum Beezie if you came down with a lung sickness that turned fatal. And what about that tidal current? It's much too strong for you, and the bottom must be slippery. If that fool Samuel should let you go, him with all his too fervent religion, you'd be swept away in an instant. Surely, girl, the Lord doesn't want to drown you! Gilly's heart sank as the procession reached the riverbank. He tried to remember what Angel had told him of this solemn ceremony. "Fust, afore weuns goes ta de ribah," she'd said, "all de baptismal cande-edates stands up in de front ob de church. De deacon, 'e lines out de wu'ds fo' we. Axt we one by one 'bout how we gwanna libe in de sight ob de Lawd oncet we bin baptized."

In his mind, Gilly could almost hear Deacon Brown's voice. He would start out low in a singsong way. Then, as he warmed to his task, he would raise his voice an octave or two and add that characteristic quaver which gave importance to his words.

"Bruddah Mo-o-ssy," he'd say, "you belie-ee-b in de Lawd Jedus Chris'? You belie-ee-b dat 'E died on dat cross fo' ta sa-abe you, a sinnah, from de consumin' fires ob hell?"

And Brother Mossy would answer with a triumphant shout, "Yes, Lawd! Praise 'E name!"

"An' es you gwanna stop stealin' you neighbah's hawgs, Bruddah Mossy, an' pay back de debts what you owes ta po' ol' Unca Isom?"

Then Brother Mossy would look a mite uncomfortable, but he'd swallow his pride. "Gawd hab mussy," he'd say, only quieter and more humbly this time, "hain't I ben-a sinnah, Lawd. Yes, yes. A wretched sinnah, Lawd, what ben redeemed!"

Then Deacon Brown would move on to the next one in the line. "Sistah May-e, you gwanna stop frettin' an' moanin' 'bout how weak you es, an' take up de strong hand ob Jedus? You gwanna promise fo' ta serbe 'E till de day you lay down dat po' body inta de mirey clay?"

"Um-mm, yessuh, t'anks You, Lawd Jedus!" Sister Mary would cry. "I do, Lawd—I do aims to serbe You all de days ob mah life!"

Gilly couldn't help but smile to himself as he thought of the events that must have so recently transpired in that tumbled-down building they used for a church. In fact, he was almost sorry that he'd missed it all. But of course, it would never do for him to show himself. That would not have helped Angel in the least.

Nevertheless, he was determined not to miss this baptism, not even for the sake of his own safety. He'd had an uncomfortable feeling that Angel's life was in danger. It had haunted him so badly last night that he'd gotten little sleep worrying over it. A premonition, perhaps, or just his growing dislike for Samuel? Then again, maybe it was just that life had turned so sour for him. Yes, he was bitter, he had to admit it. And considering all that had happened, didn't he have a perfect right?

He wondered if Angel suspected that he was out here, hiding in the marsh grasses, watching her. When they had talked last night of her coming baptism, he'd had the oddest sensation that she really wanted him to attend. Secretly, of course, that went without saying. So he'd plucked up his courage and come.

> I want Jedus ta walk wid me,
> I want Jedus ta walk wid me,
> While I'm on dis te-edious journey,
> I want Jedus ta walk wid me.

They were singing another song now, its words more like a dirge than a hymn. It reminded Gilly of the Gullah funerals he'd attended. Ah yes, but of course, this was a sort of funeral; he remembered that now. "Weuns es gwanna be buried in baptism," Angel had said. "We es all gwanna die ta sin right dere in dat ribah, in de watery grabe. Den we rise agin, Gilly, rise to a new life dat's sweet wid hope."

"Sweet with hope!' He repeated the words several times to himself. Such simplicity she had. Unassuming. Trusting. And there were times when he wished he could have just a small bit of that kind of trust. But it was all a bunch of hogwash. Samuel and preachers of his ilk had turned delusion into a fine art. Just another form of slavery, thought Gilly. Gentler, perhaps, less demanding, but slavery nevertheless.

Without realizing it, Gilly had worked himself even closer to the river. He could hear its waters gurgling and the steady slap of the waves as they washed across the mud-soaked sand.

The line of candidates approached the riverbank. They held back a bit as Deacon Brown gingerly felt his way into the swirling water. Poking and prodding at the bottom with his long staff, slipping every so often, then catching himself with the stick, the old man worked himself cautiously downward. When he'd finally found a spot deep enough, but not too deep, he turned and raised his hand to the waiting company.

"Reb'nd Sam'l," he said with a solemnity that only the most devout could muster under such trying circumstances, "de tide, she es ebbin', an' de Lawd, 'E es waitin'." Gilly knew exactly what was happening, for Angel had explained this too. The receding tide would quickly carry away the repentants' sins. Down they would go, through the dark river waters, and far out into the ocean, there to be buried forever in its unfathomable depths.

Samuel was pulling off his shoes now and heading down to the water. If its coldness shocked him, he gave no sign of it. Indeed, Gilly knew that it would be unthinkable for Samuel to do so. Even the repentant sinners who stood shivering in the chilly morning air knew that they must not let out so much as a single gasp, or the sincerity of their conversion would be in serious question.

Finally, one by one, they stepped down into the river. One by one they were buried hurriedly in its cold waters. "I baptize dee," called out Samuel so that everyone standing on the bank could hear, "in de name ob de Fadduh, de Son, an' de Holy Ghos'."

"HALLELUJAH!" shouted the onlookers. "AMEN! PRAISE 'E NAME!"

And then it was Angel's turn. Gilly tensed as he saw her approach the slippery riverbank. One of the younger deacons reached out for her hands, but persistently clinging to her crutches, Angel ignored him.

Surely she doesn't think she must do this all by herself, thought Gilly. Every nerve in his body seemed to be strung tight as piano wire. In a minute, if he didn't force himself to stay down, he'd go running straight toward her.

Zach should be there. Yes, he should. It was he who should be helping Angel into the river. He would be of no value to her spiritually, Gilly knew that, but still he should be there. Angel didn't need moral bracing, or even mental support, for that matter. Not from Zach. She had strength enough in those areas for the two of them. What she needed now was his physical presence. And sadly, that was the one thing that Zach could not give her.

Zach truly loved Angel, Gilly knew that. But there was a part of the young black man that was incapable of giving. Something had been torn away when, as a small boy, he'd been uprooted from his family. There had been times during their childhood when Gilly had seen this void in Zach quite clearly, but back then, he had not understood its source.

And if Zach were here now, thought Gilly, watching this spectacle, *how would he react? He'd be furious, of course! He'd forget about the near-idol worship he'd had for Samuel and absolutely hate the man. Maybe he'd even see him for the charlatan he is!*

Angel was having great difficulty, for the tips of her crutches were sinking deeply into the mud and throwing her off balance. Her face had turned an ashen gray, and her lips were trembling with the biting cold of the river. Then, just as Gilly felt that he could not watch a moment longer, Samuel reached out for Angel. His big, strong arms enfolded her, lifting her clean off her feet as she handed her crutches to a nearby deacon. Gilly could see the look of concern and compassion on Samuel's face. And something else, something inscrutable that Gilly had never seen before in this so-called man of God.

Struggling to keep his balance—for the river bottom was indeed slippery and the current growing steadily stronger—Samuel shifted his weight until he found his footing. Then, looking toward the wintery sky, he shouted out the baptismal words with such force that even the reeds around Gilly seemed to echo them. And before anyone even knew what was happening, both Samuel and Angel disappeared under the waves.

There was a loud gasp from the waiting spectators. Gilly sprang upward, electrified with horror. But before he could even move from his place, Samuel erupted from the dark waters still holding Angel in his arms. *"AMEN!"* he shouted.

"PRAISE DE LAWD!" called out the people in response.

Angel's face was radiant. Still holding her securely in his arms, Samuel felt his way up the slippery embankment until he was once more on dry ground. He placed Angel gently down on her own feet. Someone wrapped a warm blanket around her. There was much hugging and crying, the people all occupied with their newfound joy.

Gilly stood there, fully exposed, having totally forgotten about the necessity to hide. No one seemed to notice him, not even Angel. He felt a strange moisture working at the corner of his eyes. Tears? Surely not. He couldn't remember when he had last cried. Why now? But he knew. Oh yes, he knew. Never before had he felt so totally alone.

He was just ready to turn and walk away when he suddenly felt a hand on his shoulder. Startled, he spun around. There stood Samuel, looking down at him. The black man was smiling, not maliciously, but with friendly warmth. Gilly could say nothing. He could only stand there, dumbstruck with shock, fear coursing through him like ice through his veins.

"Massa Gilly," Samuel said. His voice was kind. "Praise Gawd dat you es safe." There was a tremor there, too, as though Samuel was nearly overcome with emotion. Then, grasping him in his great arms, the black preacher pulled Gilly close to his chest. "I heard 'bout you escape from Hilty Head. Dey said you was dead, drownt in de sea, but I know betta den dat."

"You did!" answered Gilly, his voice barely raised over a whisper. "How?"

" 'Cause de Lawd gabe me a dream, an' I seen you. I prayed fo' you, son, prayed so hard dat et hurt. Den, afta Jim died, I— I understood jes' what had happened. I figured dat Angel an' Zach was hiddin' you someplace 'pon Coosaw. Eben 'spected et was at dat ol' Praise House in de woods."

Again Gilly was at a loss for words. He could barely comprehend what Samuel was saying, but somehow the fear started slipping away.

"Don' worry, son," continued Samuel. "Your hiddin' place is safe wid me. I come out ta visit wid you sometime—" he hesitated and studied Gilly's face—"effen you wants me, dat es."

Gilly swallowed hard and nodded. Then, with a shiver of new fear, he glanced over Samuel's shoulder at the knot of people still gathered on the riverbank. No one seemed to be looking his way. They were bundling themselves up against the cold. Several started drifting away, singing spirituals, talking and chattering with happiness.

"Dey haben' seen you, Massa Gilly," Samuel assured him. "Dey's too filled up wid de Holy Sp'rit ta eben notice you standin' he'e."

"You love her!" said Gilly, surprising even himself with this sudden revelation. "You love Angel, don't you, Samuel?"

Samuel only shrugged his shoulders and sighed. "She's Zach's gal, Gilly," he said, his voice gone suddenly flat and quiet. "Et's de Lawd what I lobe."

"Yes, I see that, and I don't deny that it's true—not now." Gilly couldn't believe the words that were coming from his own mouth. It was as though some great hand had suddenly loosened his tongue and unblinded his eyes so that he could see plainly what had been there all along. "But—you—you're," he stumbled with the words. "But you're still a mortal man, Samuel, and you do love her."

Samuel dropped his eyes from Gilly's. His hands were trembling, and not from the cold. "She's Zach's gal," he repeated, this time with more determination.

Gilly reached out and clasped Samuel's cold hands. "That's all right," he said. "Your secret is safe with me."

Samuel lifted his head. They looked into each other's eyes, hesitated, and then both of them broke out into gentle laughter.

"Not so very different under the skin, are we?" observed Gilly.

"No, suh," answered Samuel. "Not so bery different at all!"

Chapter 4

Sweet Land of Liberty
(January 1, 1863)

People had come from all over the islands, for this was to be a rare celebration. It was New Year's Day, 1863, and at Camp Saxton on Port Royal Island, a festive mood filled the air. Workers had set up a large platform for the speakers and had decorated it with red, white, and blue bunting. Arrangements had been made to bring the outer island visitors across the river on barges and transports. A great barbecue pit had been dug into the ground, though there were no "fatted calves" to be had, only some lean and scraggly cattle to feed an always-hungry army. But there was plenty of molasses and corn bread. Stored produce had been collected from the surrounding plantations. The meal would be sufficient, if not sumptuous.

Zach stood in the mess hall entranceway and admired himself in the cracked peer glass that had been propped up against the rough boards of the wall. The mirror had once stood in some grand planter's home and looked rather out of place in the spartan environment of the mess hall. But it served the same purpose, nevertheless. Surely the image of no prouder man had ever been reflected from its silvered depths.

Zach had polished his boots until they reflected his face. He had a brand-new uniform, courtesy of the United States government, and it fit his tall frame splendidly. The blue jacket featured wide shoulders and clean lines. Bright gold buttons sparkled on its front. A black leather band across his chest sported the metal badge of the U.S. Infantry. The matching leather belt that held his cartridge pack encircled his waist. Below the jacket he wore the bright scarlet Zouave pants that marked his regiment as a distinct element of the Union Army's Department of the South.

Zach was proud of his uniform. He was proud to know that he was a member of the first black regiment ever to be mustered into the United States Army. Initially, the First South Carolina Volunteers was made up entirely of former slaves from the Sea Islands. But within a few months of its formation, other escaped slaves from Georgia and Florida began to join up also.

Technically, their freedom was still in question. There had been no official proclamations from the President on the matter. During the previous year, Congress had passed two Confiscation Acts that declared that any slaves who somehow managed to escape from persons "engaged in rebellion against the government of the United States" or those lucky enough to find themselves living in areas occupied by Federal forces were "forever free of their servitude."

It had been a start but had not gone nearly far enough, for there were some who questioned the legal strengths of the Confiscation Acts. In September of 1862, President Lincoln had signed a preliminary emancipation proclamation, but it, too, lacked the teeth that would be needed to enforce such a revolutionary change. Slavery had held its vicious way for so long on American soil that now it would take strong measures and much bloodshed to abolish it.

Zach stepped out into the bright sunshine of this new morning of a new year and let his gaze fall upon the long lines of glistening white tents that spread across what had once been a cotton field of the Smith Plantation. White army tents were better than white cotton, he thought to himself. The land was fertile, he could see that, but farming was far from his mind. Somehow this military encampment looked so right here.

The bitter feelings that Zach had harbored for the army after his aborted episode with General Hunter's forced enlistment had all but disappeared. He knew there were still some of his people who wanted nothing to do with the military. General Hunter had meant well when he had rounded up the able-bodied freedmen of the islands and unceremoniously shipped them all down to the fort on Hilton Head.

Zach would never forget the horror of that night. The wide-eyed fear of the men as they faced armed soldiers. The terrified screams of the women and children as they watched their menfolk being marched away.

He gave a quick jerk to the hem of his uniform jacket and pulled himself erect. Well, that was all over and done with. He couldn't let the past destroy what promised to be a bright and entirely satisfying future.

Angel's sweet face flashed through his mind. She'd be here today. Everyone who could possibly crowd on board the *Flora*, General Saxton's personal steamer, would come down from Coosaw. Since early morning, the small vessel had plowed up and down the waterways, bringing whites and blacks alike to the grove of live oaks where the festivities were to be held.

Some of the missionaries from the new school at Saint Helena Island's Oaks Plantation were already here. Zach smiled to himself at the thought of them. They had done well, these displaced Northerner zealots. They had adjusted easily to the gentle southern climate. The steady expansion of the black regiment had taken the edge off their fears of being attacked by the always-menacing might of the Confederacy.

One day last month, while on a three-day leave, he had taken Angel over to Saint Helena. There, they had met a woman by the name of Laura Towne. There had been nothing spectacular in the event, not in Zach's estimation, but Angel had been radiant with excitement over meeting Miss Towne. The two had taken to each other immediately, and by the end of the visit, they had hatched all kinds of plans.

Later in the month, Angel was to begin attending classes at Oaks Plantation, or the Penn School, as it was now being called. She longed to further the education that, thanks to Laura May Weldon, she had secretly begun during her childhood.

There would be some problems, of course. The distance was too far for Angel to travel on a daily basis, so she would have to board at one of the center's dormitories on weekdays. That meant her only time at home would be weekends. Who would care for Maum Beezie during her absence? For a while, Angel had actually considered giving up her plans, for she adamantly insisted that Maum Beezie's well-being took priority over even her most cherished dreams.

But it was Maum Beezie herself who had set the final wheels in motion. "What you talkin' 'bout, chil'? Since when do dis ol' 'omans need a nu'semaid?"

Angel had been gentle in responding to her grandmother. "Now, Maum Beezie," she had said, "dere's not a pusson on dis place what don' know how impo'tant you always ben ta takin' care ob uddah folks's needs. But you rheumatism's ben so bad lately. Why, it takes all you got jes' ta lifts you hind foots off de floor."

Maum Beezie knew Angel was right, of course. As of late, she spent most of her time in bed. Even hobbling over to her rocking chair by the hearth was a painful and exhausting expedition. Jim's death, and the efforts of his burial, had plumb taken the last bits of starch right out of her. Still, she'd never been a quitter, and nothing was more vital to her than Angel's education.

"Honey lamb, 'members way back when you an' Laura May was small? 'Members when I used ta lifts all two ob you 'pon mah lap so's ta rock you ta sleep?"

"Yes, Maum Beezie, how could I eber fo'get dat!"

"Dere was a song I used ta sing ta you den. A song 'bout de lambs an' de sheep."

Angel began to hum out loud. How familiar and beloved that old spiritual was. Spontaneously, the two women began to sing together:

> De ol' sheep done know de road,
> De ol' sheep done know de road,
> De ol' sheep done know de road,
> De young lambs mus' find de way.

"Um-hmm," said Maum Beezie, "dat was de song all right. An' dem wu'ds, dey say de same t'ing now as dey said den."

She hesitated and rubbed at her painful knees. "You gwanna hafta finds you own way in dis wu'ld, honey lamb, 'specially now. Et's a diffunt wu'ld from de one I knowed. De colu'd folks, dey's gwanna be free. Hain't too many impo'tant t'ings dis ol' 'omans gots in she haid 'ceptin' dis one. Angel, you gotsta get youse'f de best edeecation you kin gets. You gots ta stuff you head wid readin' an' writtin' an' whatsomeber else good you kin find. Den, someday right soon, you es gwanna be able ta hold up dat head wid de best ob de white folks. I seen it cumin', honey lamb. I seen it cumin' way back den when you was fu'st bo'n."

Zach had been standing silently in the shadowy corner of the old woman's cabin during this touching exchange. Never had he come so close to showing his emotions as then. Angel was too good for him, he recognized that now. She was much brighter than he was and certainly more ambitious. And he was a soldier, totally committed to a trade that in wartime made for few old bones.

Sighing, Zach walked down the low wooden steps. He loved Angel more than anyone else on this earth, and she loved him, he was certain of that. But every time they had come down to making some kind of a lasting commitment, other events had intervened. Perhaps it was just not meant to be. Well, there was nothing he could do about that now. He'd just have to let life take its course. Right now, he had a dress parade to get to.

The band of the Eighth Maine Regiment struck up a lively march as people by the hundreds began to pour into the large grove of trees. It was a weather-perfect day; as warm as summer, with the sun glinting merrily off the wide Beaufort River. Latecomers were still trying to push their way in when Zach and his regiment came marching through the crowd. *What a glorious feeling!* he thought. The buttons were fairly popping off his jacket for the swelling of his chest. In perfect precision they came: rifles at their shoulders, every head turning simultaneously toward the officers and dignitaries reviewing the parade from the speakers' platform.

Commands were barked out. *SNAP! SNAP!* went their rifles as they set them at parade rest. The President's Emancipation Proclamation was read by Doctor Brisbane, a Sea Island planter who had long since freed his own slaves. When the war had come, he had remained stubbornly loyal to the Union, so his reading of this document was entirely appropriate.

Then came the grand moment when Colonel Higginson was presented with the American flag, which had been sent to the newly formed regiment by a group of New York donors. Printed programs rustled in the hands of the spectators as the ceremony went smoothly forward. The keynote speaker said his piece and turned to sit down. The next speaker began to rise. But just at that moment, something so completely spontaneous, something so appealing, began to happen that a hush fell over every white spectator in the crowd.

> My country, 'tis of thee,
> Sweet land of liberty,
> Of thee I sing.

The old black man's voice cracked and quavered, but it electrified the very air above that flag-bedecked grove. He stood there, his hat in his work-roughened hands, his tattered clothes still dusty from the field, and he sang. People looked down at their programs but could find nothing printed there about this solo presentation. Then, understanding, they turned to look at each other, tears running freely down their faces. Other voices joined in now, all of them coming from the throats of men and women who had, until so recently, been slaves. A few of the white dignitaries on the platform started to join in, but Colonel Higginson waved them into silence.

> Land where my fathers died,
> Land of the pilgrim's pride,
> From ev-'ry mountain side,
> Let free-dom ring.

It was a moment so poignant, so charged with emotion, that every speech thereafter was completely eclipsed. Colonel Higginson tried to talk, but he found himself constantly gulping back tears. General Saxton stood up and gave his speech, but he kept it simple, for he, too, felt entirely humbled by what had just happened. In other places throughout America, on this same auspicious day, the Emancipation Proclamation was being read to waiting crowds, but nowhere—absolutely nowhere—did it hold such deep significance as here on South Carolina's wide sweep of Sea Islands.

From that point on, everything was anticlimactic. Zach stood in line to get his share of watered-down molasses and a plate full of sweet corn bread with a small helping of tough, stringy beef. Something had happened in his heart on this day. He had lost it. Not to Angel, who sat in the shade, patiently awaiting his return. No, not even to her. Zach had lost his heart and mind to his new country, for now it was truly his. And the uniform that he wore made it all the more vital that he devote every ounce of energy to this new allegiance.

Perhaps Angel sensed this as she sat in the shadows and watched his tall, lean-shouldered frame move along through the crowd. This was not the fatherless slave boy she had known as a child. Nor was he the hesitant, angry youth reaching out for human love. He was hers no longer; perhaps he had never been hers. Tears welled up in her eyes, and her throat felt so tight that she could barely breathe. What was to become of her now? she wondered. What would become of her if Zach never returned?

Chapter 5

Out ob de Mucky Mire

(Early Summer, 1863)

Angel stuffed her books into the shoulder pack she used so that she might still have enough freedom to handle her crutches. It was Friday afternoon, and she was going home to Coosaw. A thrill went through her, for an exciting change was in the offing. Maum Beezie had been carefully apprised of the situation, and as always, had readily consented. After a restful few weeks at home, Angel would be going into Beaufort, there to begin her training at one of the military hospitals. Her nursing talents had finally been recognized.

Angel's last few months at the Penn School had been happy ones. She had learned quickly and well, and to her surprise, even her speech was changing. The "bad English" of her Gullah tongue was slowly being replaced by more proper pronunciations. Still, she chuckled to herself when she thought of this, for Gullah came back to her quickly enough when she was alone with her own people. Indeed, Angel was determined to hold onto the colorful and descriptive sayings of her Gullah heritage rather than the more mundane ones of the whites. "Day clean" held far more meaning than "sunrise." "Callin' de wind" was infinitely more picturesque than "fanning the rice." And "hist de windah" came easier to her mouth than "open the window."

Miss Laura Towne had been the soul of patience with Angel

during these past few months. There were those who had said that the black girl's twisted feet made her a poor candidate for advanced schooling. It had hurt Angel deeply when she had heard it.

"Can you believe it?" said Laura to her friend Ellen Murray. The two teachers had been called into the superintendent's office to give him their thoughts on the matter. "One would hope that we had gotten past such foolishness by now. It's like saying a man has less brain power because he's got black skin. I thought we'd come down here to do away with such blind prejudice."

Laura Towne and Ellen Murry, both of them college graduates and women of exceptional talent, had already proven that they were as capable as any of their male counterparts when it came to this enterprise known as the Port Royal Experiment. And now Laura found herself fighting for a new cause. Why should a physical handicap stop a young woman from doing what her talents so obviously fitted her for? No, she was on Angel's side completely. If the girl wanted to be a nurse, then so be it. And no amount of hindrance or compromise should be placed in her way.

Grateful for the chance she was about to receive, Angel immediately began plotting and planning. Maum Beezie would still need to be cared for. Not a difficult assignment, she decided, for the old woman was completely undemanding. Then there was Gilly. Samuel had done admirably well in caring for Gilly on the weekdays while Angel was away at school. Tentatively at first, then by leaps and bounds, Samuel and Gilly's friendship had once more begun to flower.

As for Zach, well, Angel was beyond worrying about him. He was so wrapped up in his new military career that she seldom saw him. His body had become muscle-bound and hard, his carriage ramrod stiff, and his face—Angel couldn't quite describe Zach's face. There was something in his eyes that she had never seen before. Cold and distant? It was hard to say. In any event, when they were together, which was seldom now, they had little to say to each other.

One evening, well after the sun had sunk behind the loblolly pines, Samuel had come back to Maum Beezie's cabin after an especially long session with Gilly. Stretching himself out on the rocking chair that stood in front of the chimney place, he surveyed the fire's dying embers. Maum Beezie was asleep, finally comfortable after a tortuous day with her rheumatism. Lifting a poker to stir the glowing coals, Samuel let out a deep sigh.

" 'E wants ta go," he said simply.

Occupied with her books, Angel had barely heard Samuel's low comment. She hesitated, then looked up. "Did you say sumpin', Sam'l?"

"I said, 'e wants ta go—ta leabe Coosaw."

"Gilly? Are you talkin' 'bout Gilly?"

"Mm-hm." Samuel stared at the small flame he had brought to life.

"Nuttin' new 'bout dat," answered Angel. Unconcerned, she went back to her reading.

"Dis time dere es. 'E wants me ta take 'e ta Savannah."

"Savannah? What fo'?"

"Tattnall's down dere. So's he Mosquito Fleet."

Commodore Josiah Tattnall had been Gilly's commanding officer back before he had been wounded and taken captive. The little "Mosquito Fleet," as the embryo of the Confederate Navy had been called, was still in existence. Having done little more than pester the great Union armada that had taken Port Royal Sound early in the war, the original title for the odd assortment of small river steamers had somehow stuck.

"But—how do Gilly know 'bout dat?" Angel still felt a certain mistrust for the former master's son. Accordingly, she had become very circumspect when she talked with Gilly and had warned Samuel to do the same.

"I done tol' 'e," answered Samuel honestly.

"Oh!" said Angel. There was an accusing tone in her voice that caused Samuel to wince.

"Mm-hmm," he answered. "Time dat boy went back ta 'e own peoples, Angel." He placed the poker back in its rack. "Effen

Gilly stays 'lone out in dat woods much longer, 'e mind's gwanna go as chirpy as a June bug's."

"You wan' him ta go back ta de wah, Sam'l? You wan' him ta start fightin' fo' de Seceshes all oba ag'in?"

Samuel was quiet for some time before answering. "Et's de best t'ing, Angel. Effen 'e stay holed up he'e at Coosaw fo' de rest ob de wah, 'e never gwanna be able ta look at 'eself in de mirror agin."

Angel frowned, then nodded. Samuel was right, and she knew it. "Um-hm," she said slowly, "I ben-a t'inkin' 'bout dat." She glanced over at Maum Beezie to make sure that the old woman was asleep. "But how es we gwanna get Gilly away from Coosaw, Sam'l? Dem Union so'diers es eberywhere."

Samuel sniffed and shifted his weight. "Shouldn' be all dat hard," he said. "Harriet might could do et. She's gwanna be back in a few weeks—you know." Samuel had great faith in Harriet Tubman, the well-loved emancipator, whom he knew on a first-name basis. To many of the blacks, Harriet was a second Moses. "Effen anybody kin he'p us," said Samuel quietly, "she kin."

Angel shook her head. "But would she, Sam'l? I mean, Gilly— 'e's a white man an' a Secesh at dat. You know how Harriet feels 'bout Seceshes." Angel shook her head again. There was doubt written all over her face. "De trut' es, Sam'l, I don' know effen we kin eben trus' Harriet when et comes ta Gilly."

Samuel scratched at his chin. "Let me t'ink 'pon dat some. Meantime, don' you fret you haid none. I done tol' you I was gwanna takes care ob Gilly, an' I meant et."

Angel smiled at Samuel. As of late, he had come to be such a good friend. And though he was considerably older than she was, Angel had not failed to notice Samuel's broad shoulders and fine physique.

Samuel was as good as his word. He continued to make numerous trips to the old Praise House in the woods, each time bringing with him food, medicines, and even some books that Angel had managed to find in what had once been the library of the Big House. Gilly was stronger now, and his mental state, though still somewhat tenuous, seemed to improve as his trip to Savannah became more of a reality. He constantly talked of what he would do when he got back with his old comrades.

But the situation with Gilly came to a head much sooner than either Samuel or Angel ever imagined it would, and all because of an old nemesis from their plantation days. They had seen neither hide nor hair of Cudjo, the Weldon Oaks' former slave driver, since Samuel had run him off the place shortly after the Union's takeover. Then one day in mid-June, a riverboat carrying a large and official-looking contingent tied up at the Coosaw docks.

The usual number of military men and government officials disembarked. Behind them came a crowd of men whom Angel had never seen before. "Land speculators from de Nort'!" Samuel hissed in her ear. In the midst of them stood Cudjo.

He was dressed fit to kill in pin-striped pants, a fawn waistcoat, and a gray, silk ascot tied meticulously at his neck. A silver stickpin glinted from the ascot. It held an amethyst as large as a man's knuckle. Perched on Cudjo's head was a fine beaver top hat, gray to match the ascot. It was adorned with a black silk band. He looked fit and prosperous, and they were soon to find out why.

Land sales of the properties "abandoned" by the Southern planters and their families were fast turning into a lucrative business. After the Emancipation Proclamation, opportunists and speculators poured into the area. Never one to miss out on a good thing, Cudjo had set to work acquiring as much land as he could possibly get his hands on.

It was still not easy for blacks to buy land. Most of the plantations' former slaves found themselves either ousted or working for hire on property being gobbled up by Northern land buyers. A few, with encouragement from the government, had managed to purchase four or five acres of farmland and a plot of ground for their homes. But it was difficult to compete with the money-rich speculators who swarmed across the confiscated lands like devouring locusts.

Cudjo was better off than most. Early on, he had made friends with some well-placed government officials. And as tainted as his money was—for there were a host of stories about his dishonest business dealings—it spent just as well as anyone else's greenbacks.

Now, it seemed, Cudjo wanted land on Coosaw. His desire stemmed from a series of old insults that he was determined to collect upon. Cudjo hated Maum Beezie. He hated Samuel. Most of all, he hated Angel. Each of them had managed to outsmart him at one time or another. But Angel, being no more than a "chit of a niggra gal" as he was wont to call her, especially raised his ire.

And to Angel's dismay, the land Cudjo wanted was the very piece of property upon which she and Maum Beezie had their little cabin. It was heavily wooded and of no value for farming, but none of this mattered to Cudjo. Within sight of the cabin were the old plantation slave quarters still occupied by a half-dozen families. Cudjo wanted to buy that land too. Just why, he didn't say, but Angel could guess.

Alarmed by Cudjo's brazenness, she went immediately to Mr. Philbrick, a prominent plantation superintendent and more recently an acting agent for interested investors. Philbrick was a sharp-witted but compassionate man. He had seen the growing plight of the former slaves and had thought to help them by himself purchasing large tracts of land. Then, for reasonable sums and with generous terms, he allowed the freedmen to buy directly from him whatever acres they could afford. It was an equitable plan, but for Angel, it had one catch. Philbrick dealt only with the male heads of families.

Would Mr. Philbrick understand her needs? As Angel wondered, she realized it was a chance she must take. She had no delusions as to what Cudjo would do once he got hold of her and Maum Beezie's little plot of earth.

As it happened, on the day that Angel arrived at Mr. Philbrick's headquarters, the two missionary women, Laura Towne and Ellen Murry, were also visiting. And once again, it was these two brave women who intervened on Angel's behalf.

"They *are* a family, Mr. Philbrick," insisted Laura Towne,

"despite the fact that no males are present. And as surely as there is a God in heaven, that land should be theirs! Who, may I ask, has a better right to it? Would you put an old woman and a crippled child out in the cold for a handful of shekels?" Despite her earlier insistence that Angel's physical handicaps should not be considered a hinderance, Laura was not above exploiting them if the cause was right!

Fidgeting nervously in his seat, after a speech like this Mr. Philbrick could do nothing less than grant the girl's simple request. Angel produced her carefully horded bit of money as a down payment. With the price at $1.25 an acre, she could do little more than buy just the property the house sat on and its adjacent garden plot. But feeling suddenly generous, especially under the hot stares of the two missionary women, Mr. Philbrick agreed to hold in trust at least four more acres of wooded land for a period of two years.

Angel was exuberant when she returned home that night. But when Cudjo got wind of the deal that had been cut, he was too furious for words. Then and there, he decided that he must, once and for all, do in this black girl who had so plagued his life.

It would remain a complete mystery to both Angel and Samuel how Cudjo found out about Gilly. But the old saying "money talks" was obviously at work. When an investigator from the provost marshal's office showed up at their door on a warm Thursday morning, Angel knew that real trouble was brewing.

"It has come to our attention," said the provost marshal with sternness written into his every feature, "that you and your grandmother are harboring an escaped Confederate prisoner of war. Surely I need not tell you what could happen if you are found guilty of such a crime."

Maum Beezie, lying propped up in her bed, went directly to the heart of the matter. "I spect' et was dat polecat Cudjo what tol' you such t'ings, Massa Yank. Dat man, 'e kin lie better den a one-legged dawg wid a tick in 'e foot. Spect 'e hain't tol' you dat 'e's plottin' fo' ta take dis cabin 'way from weuns. Mm-mm, et sho es a sorry day when you all listens ta de rabin's ob a niggra wearin' a silber toofpick at 'e neck."

Startled and put completely off balance by this tirade from the elderly black woman, the provost officer decided to make a hasty retreat—at least for the time being. "We'll have to do some further investigating into this matter," he said as he backed his way toward the door. "I'm sure that you understand the necessity for this, my dear. It's not that we're trying to put you out of your home—" He never had time to finish the last sentence.

"GET OUT!" shouted Maum Beezie. "An' effen you keep dealin' wid polecats, den don' you nebah come back!"

Angel had to smile at this. It was seldom that Maum Beezie lost her temper, but look out when she did! Nodding curtly, Angel bid the provost officer a hasty farewell. Still, she knew that Maum Beezie had done little, if anything, to diffuse the situation. And now she was certain that there must be no further delay in getting Gilly off Coosaw. Yes, she decided, it would have to be done with all dispatch—possibly even tonight.

As luck would have it, Zach came home the very next day and announced that he'd been granted a three-day pass. Angel told him of Cudjo's sudden appearance, of his plans to buy the plot of land they lived on, and of her going to see Mr. Philbrick. She told him that Samuel had managed to spirit Gilly away during the darkest part of last night. By now, she assured him, they should be well on their way to Savannah.

Zach's face turned first stormy, then inscrutable. He said nothing.

"Et's all right now, Zach. Mistah Philbrick done take care ob eberyt'ing fo' we. We es finally out ob all dis mucky mire."

"No you hain't," said Zach, his voice threateningly low. "Mistah Philbrick, 'e hain't cleaned up all de mucky mire."

Angel was startled. Zach seemed to have something in mind, but she couldn't imagine what.

Giving her a stormy look, Zach finally said, "Et's time ta do what's ben needed doin' fo' a long time wid dat good-fo'-nuttin' snake. You t'ink, jes' 'cause you bought dis land, dat 'e's gwanna go 'way? Uh-uh, hain't gwanna happin'. 'E jes' find anuder way ta makes you mis'able."

"Wha—what should I do, Zach?"

"Nuttin'!" He was very emphatic. "Dis time, et's me what's gwanna do et."

"But—"

"Don't axe me no mo' ques'ions, gal." And with that, he stomped out of the house.

By evening, Zach had still not returned. Angel was terribly worried, but there was nothing she could do.

When Zach left Coosaw that day, he headed straight for the ferry crossing that went from Ladies Island to Beaufort. He knew where Cudjo lived, but first he had another piece of work to do. An old friend of his, a black man who had declined to join the regiment of the First South Carolina Volunteers, lived on the western outskirts of town. Grady was a shifty sort of fellow. He had belonged to a north Florida planter who had badly mistreated his slaves. Grady had managed to escape and come here to the Port Royal area, but he had a chip on his shoulder ten feet wide.

Like Cudjo, thought Zach. Just like Cudjo. Well, that was all right. Sometimes it took a varmint to catch a varmint. Grady was like Cudjo in another way too. He was an active practitioner of the arts of voodoo. Zach could never forget how Cudjo had carved those horrid little images, then given them to both him and Gilly when they were just boys. Cudjo had tried to trick Gilly into playing a part in his black magic schemes. It had all backfired, but Cudjo never seemed to learn. Well, he would this time, decided Zach. He definitely would learn this time.

Grady was pleased to see him. They talked for a while. Some money passed hands. "Should be easy 'nuff," said Grady. "I knows dis yellah niggra 'omans what libes on Cat Island. She goes ta visit Cudjo on a reg'lar basis, 'long wid some uddah ob she male frien's." Grady was smiling.

"Will she do et?" asked Zach, his face very intense.

"Fo' a price," answered Grady.

Zach dug back in his pocket and pulled out a few more bills. "When?" he asked.

"Kyan't say," answered Grady. "Maybe dis week. Maybe nex'. All depen' 'pon Cudjo."

Not more than a week later, Zach heard the news. Cudjo was dead. He'd been found lying on the floor in the rooms that he rented. A grotesque little figure, a rare likeness of Cudjo made of hemp and clay, hung suspended from the ceiling at the foot of his bed. Stuck in its body, run clear through it, in fact, was Cudjo's silver stickpin.

Cudjo himself had not a mark on him. He lay in a twisted pile on the floor with a look of horror on his face as though he had died in a great spasm of pain. Some suspected poison, though not a trace of it could be found. Others, the black folks mostly, simply shook their heads knowingly. Cudjo had had a spell put on him, they said, a voodoo curse so powerful that he had simply died of fright.

Zach smiled to himself when he heard this. It would take a lot of weeks to earn all the money that he had borrowed, but the debt would be paid. If there was one thing Zach had learned in his difficult years of growing up, it was this: A man eventually must pay for whatever he has done in his life, and Cudjo had just paid his debt.

Chapter 6

Fields of Endless Days

(Summer 1863)

Stepping gingerly across a puddle, with one crutch pressed hard against her side for balance, Angel tried to negotiate the blighted ground that had once been the rose garden of the Weldons' stately Beaufort home. She stopped to catch her breath, then lifted her eyes to look toward the house. What a sad sight it was! Unpainted, rough-hewn boards had been nailed helter-skelter across broken sections of siding. The wisteria vine, which by early summer normally would have engulfed the east side of the house with dangling blossoms, now lay in a browning heap at the base of the chimney. Overgrown weeds choked out the cassena bushes by the porch railing, and the front walkway was virtually nonexistent.

Saddest of all was the China berry tree. It had been hacked and chopped at by sabers and swords and obviously used repeatedly for target practice. In her mind's eye, Angel could still see young Gilly leaning out of his bedroom window to pluck off sticky berries from the tree's widespread branches. If he were in a particularly devilish mood, which was often the case, Gilly delighted in pelting anyone foolish enough to come within his range. His favorite victim was Josephine, the family cook, for her protests often became loud and hilarious. And the more Josephine squealed, the more daring Gilly would become in his "berry" attacks.

The smile brought on by remembering past events soon faded, however, for the house Angel now saw had little in common with the one stored away in her childhood memories. This building was nothing short of a wreck. It desperately needed a coat of paint. Where once a slim piazza had graced the second-floor level, there was now only an ugly scar. Torn away for firewood, thought Angel. The very idea of such wanton destruction made her angry. Beaufort was full of scavengers, some poor and desperately in need, others just greedy. Sadly, the latter were often numbered among the highest-ranking government and military officials now occupying the town.

Despite its sad state of disrepair, Angel could see that the Weldon house was still in use. Soldiers lounged on the front porch, their booted feet propped up on the dilapidated railing. The doorways, which had led out onto the upper piazza, had been boarded over for safety, but there was a constant buzzing sound coming through the windows, as though every room and even the hallways were filled to capacity. And if she listened hard enough, Angel could also hear the sounds of moaning or the sudden cry of someone in pain. It was obvious that the building's present purpose had little to do with family life, for like many another Beaufort mansion, the Weldon house had been turned into a military hospital.

Just a block or two away was the Daner house, and it was this dwelling that was Angel's destination. But since she had had to pass the Weldon house anyway, it seemed a shame not to take a closer look at it. Now she was sorry that she had done so. Perhaps it would have been better to have left her happy memories of the house intact.

Shrugging off her despondency, Angel continued across the lawn until she reached the roadway. She came to the corner and headed north toward Craven Street. There were soldiers everywhere, many of them, like herself, hobbling along on crutches. All of Beaufort had become a hospital town. She nodded and smiled at those whom she passed. There were few who responded. Most simply turned away, as though the sight of a crippled black girl was somehow repulsive. Angel didn't mind.

She was used to such reactions and had long ago learned to live with them.

But when she finally did reach Craven Street, she felt a thrill of excitement that no amount of snubbing could dampen. There was the Daner house, its white siding as dilapidated as any other dwelling. But lounging on the front lawn and sitting on the open porch were more black soldiers than she had seen in months. Many were wounded and heavily bandaged. There were men who had been blinded and a large number of amputees. One poor fellow sat alone, on the bottom porch step. He was crying to himself, but no one seemed to pay him the least bit of mind.

It was all so terribly pathetic, thought Angel, but yes, it was also heartening in a way. This home was the first one in Beaufort to be specifically designated as a hospital for the "contraband" soldiers. Heretofore, the black men wounded in battle had had no such place to care for them. It had been a disgraceful state of affairs, considering how bravely these men had fought.

It was here that Angel was to begin her nursing duties. But the closer she came to the house, the more her excitement ebbed away. There seemed to be so many wounded men lying about. Why, there were even pallets for them on the open porches! How was she to manage in such overcrowded conditions? Would her crippled feet make her too awkward? Would the doctors and the other nurses think her unfit?

Trying to rekindle a spark of courage, Angel hesitated in the roadway and thought back to what she'd heard of the battles now raging in Charleston harbor. The bombardment of that proud city had been going on for weeks, with little more to show for it than an alarming number of dead and wounded Union soldiers. They had fought their way onto a sand spit called Morris Island, and after receiving a murderous pounding, had taken an insignificant earthwork called Fort Wagner.

Every day, another boatload of battle casualties returned to Hilton Head. The worst of the wounded, the white ones, at least, were kept there until they could be safely brought over to Beaufort. Not so with the Negro soldiers. They were promptly transported to one of the two already-crowded contraband hospitals in the city, and if they died in the process— Angel cut off that final thought because it made her angry.

"De colo'd so'diers es bein' used fo' cannon fodder," Samuel had complained, and now Angel knew that he was right. If the federal government had once questioned its need for inducting Negroes into the Union Army, the ongoing battle for Charleston had certainly been a positive factor in changing its mind!

All this went through Angel's mind as she slowly surveyed the contraband hospital house. But she realized that there was no time for bitterness. An important task loomed before her, a task that, if it were to be done properly, would require her complete commitment. And to that end, she knew she must put aside all feelings of anger and frustration.

Readjusting her crutch and hoisting up the small bundle she was carrying, Angel started up the walkway to the Daner house. She was almost to the steps when a small black woman stepped out through the open doorway. Walking to the railing, the woman leaned over it and tossed out what appeared to be a bucketful of bloody water. Still unaware of the watching girl, the woman slumped wearily against a post and began to mop her face with her badly stained apron.

"Harriet!" Angel happily cried out the woman's name, for she had recognized her immediately.

Harriet Tubman was by now a well-known figure in Beaufort. Her humanitarian efforts with the Underground Railroad were legendary. She had brought down upon herself the wrath of the Confederate government, so much so that there was a high price on her head. But this had only furthered her fame with the contrabands of the Port Royal area. She was loved and respected by the blacks and whites alike, though only a select few knew that Harriet was also a very capable Union spy.

And now, as though all of her other undertakings were not sufficient, Harriet had volunteered to serve as a nurse in the contraband hospital. Not surprisingly, she was doing the most degrading of duties—cleaning out slop buckets, scrubbing floors, and bathing the wounded. Nothing seemed too hard or too menial for this brave-hearted little woman.

Moving as fast as her crippled feet would allow, Angel mounted the steps and flung her arms around Harriet. "Oh, Harriet, et sho' es good ta see you!"

And as bone-weary as she was, Harriet responded with a greeting equally as warm. "He'e chil'," she said after kissing both of Angel's cheeks, "push dat lazy so'dier boy offen de rocky chair an' set youse'f down. You look plum tuckered out!"

"Only effen you set down fust, Harriet. By-de-by, was dat a bucket ob bloody watah I saw you dumpin' in de yaad?"

Harriet frowned. "Mmm," she answered, a scowl indenting her brow. "I sta'ts fo' ta wash de mud offen deese po' boys, onliest ta discober dat what dey es caked wid hain't mud at all!"

Angel nodded. "Miz Towne took me ober ta Hilty Head so's I could get mah papers ta come he'e ta Bofo't. Met a 'omans dere name ob Clara Barton. She done tol' us some ob how bad et's ben up dere in Cha'ston."

Harriet shook her head sadly. "Effen anysomebody knows, honey chil', et be Mizz Clara. Hab you heard any ob dem stories 'bout how she got de whole U.S. A'my riled up?"

Angel nodded. She had heard a few things, but she could see that Harriet was just bursting to tell her more. It was amazing to see that as famous and brave a woman as Harriet was, she could still get excited about the exploits of others. Realizing that Harriet desperately needed to get off her feet for a while, Angel decided to indulge her. Patting the chair next to hers, Angel asked Harriet to sit down and relate what she knew of Clara Barton. There was an immediate gathering around of those on the porch, for the soldiers loved to hear about the brave woman who had shown them such care and compassion.

"Dey call Mizz Barton," Harriet began, "Angel ob de Battlefield, an' fo' a mighty good reason too." All of the listening men vigorously nodded their heads in agreement.

"I he'e tell dat et all sta'ted up dere where I come from—de state ob Maryland or dere 'bouts. Et was durin' de battles ob

Fredericksburg an' Antietam dat Mizz Barton come by dat name. Terrible times dey was! Why, de ground was near cobered knee-deep wid all de dead an' wounded."

Then, in her own wonderful and captivating style, Harriet proceeded to fill in the details of Clara Barton's valor. Apparently unruffled by the sight of hundreds of mangled bodies, the deafening roar of the guns, and the screams of dying men and horses, Clara had done her work efficiently and well. She had been appalled by the horrible conditions at the army field hospitals and had complained long and loud over the lack of trained ambulance crews for removing the wounded. Thus she was determined that these battles would not be a repeat of what had happened at places like Bull Run.

Angel listened to all of this with a growing horror. No wonder Clara Barton was so fanatical about establishing adequate field hospitals and training emergency personnel to work under the pressures of battle conditions. She and others like her had vowed to bring about a change in the way the army ran its medical corps. Fredericksburg and Antietam had been the start of that change. And now Miss Barton was determined to carry her work even farther.

At Hilton Head, Angel had met numerous officials of the civilian-run Sanitary Commission. She was told, by way of an introduction to her new duties, that the Sanitary Commission had been formed in June of 1861 as a check and balance to the army's surgeon general's office. Clara had been one of the first in line to seek placement in a war zone deep within the South. Port Royal and the Sea Islands seemed to be a natural choice, but there was still much opposition to her work from short-sighted army surgeons who felt that a woman had no place, as a nurse or otherwise, on or even near the field of battle.

Harriet chuckled when she told the listening group how Miss Barton had finally weaseled her way south. It had taken the special appointment of her older brother, David, to the Sanitary Commission on Hilton Head. The fact that neither David nor his wife wanted such a questionable honor made little impression on his incomparable sister. When Clara was determined to have her way, not even family ties could deter her.

Upon first reaching Hilton Head, Clara found herself with little to do other than socialize with the officers. The Sea Islands were deceptively peaceful. But she soon discovered that it was only the calm before the storm. In July, the bombardment of Charleston began, and the bloody carnage that was to follow shocked even her battle-hardened sensibilities.

"I tells you," declared Harriet, "dat 'omans kyan't abide settin' in a rocky chair no mo' den dis po' 'omans kin!" She slapped her knee with glee and let out a loud hoot. By now, Harriet had gained quite an audience, so she played her part to the hilt. "Now mayhap you done yeddy dat Mizz Clara kin ride a hoss 'bout as good as any cav'rymens kin do. Ki, an' dat's de trut'! Why, I seen she plenty ob times ridin' wild as de wind down de beach 'pon Hilty Head. Face shinin' like de sun. Laughin' ta de sky. Hair sweepin' past she shou'ders. Um-mm, but dat ben a sight!"

"Tell 'em 'bout what she done durin' de battle fo' Fo't Wagner, Mizz Harriet," said a soldier, who, though having lost his right leg, had managed to survive the fort's first assault.

Harriet sobered then and reached out to gently touch the young infantryman. "Was you dere, son?" she asked.

Tears came to the young man's eyes. "Yessum, I was dere, sho nuff. Lost a lot ob my friends dere too," he said quietly as he glanced down at the stump of his leg. "Saw Cu'nul Shaw go down. Pitiful t'ing dat was. Somehow I drug mahse'f back ta de beach. Dat's when I fust met Mizz Barton. She save mah life, an' dat fo' true! Dem a'my doctahs say I was done fo'—no use ta waste dere time wid me. But Mizz Barton, et was like she come straight down from heaben jes' like dey say!"

Angel had been at Hilton Head when Clara Barton had returned from Charleston for a much-needed rest. She wondered if she should tell these men just how much of a toll the prolonged battle had taken on their beloved field nurse. On the verge of shell shock, her eyes injured from blowing sand and burning gunsmoke, her fair skin blistered by the broiling sun of the unprotected sand spit, Clara had not been a pretty sight to see. But the carnage of war was an old story to these men. Angel decided that they'd understand and love Miss Barton all the more for her sufferings on their behalf.

Looking down at these young infantryman, Angel felt a wave of deep compassion. Yes, what she was doing was right. Surely it didn't matter that her feet were weak and twisted, for her hands and her will were strong. She had thought that she understood what it was to be a nurse—all of those years working with Maum Beezie for the people in the quarters. But that had been nothing compared to this. Still, if women like Clara Barton and Harriet Tubman were able to overcome the host of obstacles they had had to face, then Angel could too. It was only a matter of determination.

"Well, suh," said Harriet suddenly, slapping her hands against her thighs and pushing herself out of the chair, "kyan't set 'round he'e all day crackin' we teet'." She looked down at Angel. "Dere's wuk ta be done, li'l lady."

Angel snapped out of her reverie and looked up into Harriet's twinkling eyes. It was good that they had had this talk. It was just the kind of introduction she needed to the plight of these brave men. But now she knew that she must also gain their trust. If they were ever to recuperate from their wounds and return to their families, then past battles and bitter memories must be put aside.

"De whole house es takin' up wid beds fo' de wounded," explained Harriet, her eyes darting quickly down to her apron and then back to Angel's face. "De nu'ses, weuns dat stays he'e, es libin' out back in what uset ta be de slabes 'qua'tahs. Dat hain't gwanna trouble you none, es et, missy?"

Angel laughed. "Et's gwanna feel jes' like home, Mizz Harriet!" She turned and gave the soldier nearest her a meaningful look. Understanding, he smiled back.

Lifting her head slightly, Harriet sniffed at the odors coming from the house and winced. "Smells like a hawg farm," she said disgustedly. "Gwanna hab ta get some mo' clean beddin' an' a heap lot mo' bandages. Onliest befo' you rolls up yo sleeves, Angel honey, dere's someone inside who's ben waitin' ta see you."

Angel's face lighted up with pleasure. Zach! It must be Zach! So he hadn't forgotten that she was coming to Beaufort after all. And seeing as how he was right over at Camp Shaw, surely he had managed to get a few hours of leave.

But no, when she entered the house, it was not Zach at all who stood there in the shadows smiling at her. It was Samuel. A surge of disappointment washed over her, making her feel immediately guilty. Samuel was a good friend. He always seemed to be there when she most needed him. And unlike Zach, he always had a gentle respect for her feelings. Surely it was unfair for her to be thinking of Zach now—wishing that it were he who had come to welcome her to Beaufort.

Samuel reached out his hands and lightly touched Angel's forearms. He had an odd look on his face, as though he were trying overly hard to hide some wonderful secret. "Welcome ta Bo'fort, Angel. Soon as you gets youse'f settled in, I gots some'un I wants you ta meet." Samuel's eyes were sparkling with pleasure.

Now what! thought Angel. The slight feeling of irritation at finding Samuel waiting for her rather than Zach began to fade. Something told her that an important event was about to take place—an event that might very well change the course of her life. "Don' keep me guessin', Sam'l. What's dis all about?"

"Um-mm." Samuel shook his head, but there was a mischievous smile on his face. "Not jes' yet, Angel. I ben listnin' ta you talkin' wid Harriet 'bout dat battle up near Cha'ston. Figuh you had 'nuff war talk fo' de time bein'. Jes' gets youse'f settled in he'e fust. Mayhap let Harriet show you what needs doin'. Den, afo' suppah, we two es gwanna take a walk on obah ta de Oaks house. I sho' don' wanna knocks de breaf outten you afo' you gets a chance ta kitch et in de fust place!"

Now Angel was really curious. What special secret could Samuel possibly have? Still, there was some strange bit of obstinacy in her that would not allow her to give Samuel the satisfaction of winning. So instead of pressing him further, she merely shrugged her shoulders and turned away. "Don' matter none," she said, trying to sound casual. But before she had gotten more than three steps away, she swung around and asked, "Sam'l, have you heard anyt'ing from Zach?"

Samuel's smile faltered. He dropped his gaze into his hands as though to study his nails. "Yessum," he said slowly, "I done talked ta' 'e jes' yestaday."

"Yestaday! Where es 'e, den? Why hain't 'e come obah he'e ta see me?"

Samuel looked at her pathetically. He opened his mouth to speak, then shut it again.

"Sumpin's wrong, hain't et!" A cold sweat had broken out on Angel's brow. She had visions of Zach lying wounded—maybe even dying—in some dirty, backwater place.

Samuel hesitated, tightened his jaw, then looked straight into her eyes. "Nuttin' yet," he answered, but there was obviously something threatening behind his words.

Angel reached out and grabbed Samuel's hand. "Dis hain't no time ta play me fo' a fool, Sam'l. Sumpin's wrong wid Zach, I kin tell. E's hurt er sick er—"

Samuel pressed her down into a nearby chair. "Angel, I sho wisht you hadn' askt me 'bout Zach jes' now. De trut' es, I don' know effen sumpin's wrong er not." He stopped to take a deep breath, shook his head, then hurried on. "But since you hab asked, den I gotsta tell you. Dere may be trouble 'bout Cudjo's dyin' like-a 'e done."

"Trouble?" asked Angel, alarm making her voice sound distant. "What kind ob trouble?"

Samuel sat down next to her. He pressed the tips of his fingers to his forehead and sighed. "Et's dem guberment agents, de ones Cudjo wu'ked fo'. Dey ben nosin' 'round some—askin' lots ob ques'ions."

"What kind ob ques'ions, Sam'l?"

Samuel hesitated and bit at his lower lip. Then he looked straight into Angel's eyes. "Puzactly what did Zach tell you 'e was gwanna do, Angel? What'd 'e say afta you tol' 'e 'bout Cudjo cumin' back ta trouble you an Maum Beezie?"

Angel hesitated to answer, knowing full well that what she had to say would probably implicate Zach in Cudjo's death. At first, she thought it would be best to tell Samuel nothing. After all, he was on her side, wasn't he? And even though there seemed to be a growing antagonism between the two men, Angel felt certain that Samuel would never do anything to cause Zach any real harm. Besides, Samuel had as much reason to hate Cudjo as Zach did. It was Cudjo who had played a hand in the death of Phoebe, the one woman whom Samuel had truly loved.

But Samuel kept looking at her, his eyes boring into hers, and Angel knew that she must tell him the truth. "Zach was mighty upset 'bout Cudjo comin' ta Coosaw an' makin' t'reats," she said quietly. "I tried ta tell 'e dat Mistah Philbrook had made t'ings all right, but 'e wouldn't pay me no mind. Said dat et was time ta take care ob Cudjo once an' fo' all. Said dat I shouldn' worry mah head no mo' 'bout losin' de cabin an' de land et's on."

Samuel nodded. "I taught et might a ben sumpin' like-a dat." He clenched his hands tightly together and dropped them between his knees. "Et might could take some time afo' deese guberment mens got wind ob dat, but sooner er later, dey's gwanna find out. Now, I don' say dat Zach 'zactly murdered Cudjo—"

With rising anger, Angel interrupted him. "How kin you eben t'ink such a t'ing 'bought you bes' friend?" She knew immediately that it was the wrong thing to say. She'd had her own misgivings about Zach's part in Cudjo's death. But to say it out loud like this—somehow it seemed like an awful betrayal!

Samuel was still looking straight into her eyes, and she knew that he had read her thoughts. Unbidden, tears began to trickle down her cheeks. Samuel reached out and gently brushed them away with the side of his finger. "Po' li'l Angel," he said. "You es too young fo' ta carry such heaby burdens. An' I don't blame Zach none. Haben't I said ta mahse'f a hundred times how much I wisht I could do sumpin' bad ta dat skunk, Cudjo. Et weren't Christian what I was t'inkin'—me be'n a serbant ob de Lawd an' all—but I sho done hab taught 'bout et many a time! Effen Zach done what 'e taught 'e had ta do, den dis po' sinnah kyan't judge 'e none!"

Angel looked up at Samuel then and nodded her head. "Et

was Cudjo 'ese'f what brought on de end. All dem times 'e was dabblin' wid hoodoo. 'E beliebed in black magic so much dat, in de end, et kilt him. Zach—'e only hastened et on some."

Samuel nodded his agreement. "Ebil begets ebil," he said sagely. "But dat hain't gwanna stop dem guberment mens from makin' trouble."

Now Angel was truly alarmed. "What kin we do?" she asked.

Samuel shook his head. "Nuttin'. Not fo' de time bein' anyhow. 'Sides, dere hain't a t'ing dey kin prove. Ta kill a man wid 'e own hoodoo—how es dat gwanna hold up in a court ob law?"

Angel wasn't convinced. "But dey kin make et mighty ha'd fo' Zach," she said quietly.

"Um-hm," answered Samuel. "Dat dey kin."

Somehow the brightness of the day was blighted. Angel went to inspect her new living quarters, but she dreaded having to see Samuel again, even though he had promised her a happy surprise. If Zach were in danger, nothing could possibly lift the gloom that had ascended over her heart.

Harriet Tubman walked between the rows of sick and wounded, stopping now and then to reach out to this one or lay an encouraging hand on that one. When she spoke, her voice was gentle but filled with strength. The men whom she passed knew how much she cared about them. Some grasped her hands hard and let their tears flow freely. They told her of the friends and loved ones they'd lost. They told her of their fears for the future. And to each, she gave her whole attention, assuring them when she could, simply listening when there was no assurance to be given.

Finally, Angel also turned to Harriet. Blurting out the story of Cudjo and Zach's probable part in his death, she laid out the sum total of her concerns. "What kin I do ta he'p Zach?" she asked, the tears glistening in her eyes.

"Jes' stand 'ahind 'e, Angel honey. Dat's all you kin do. An' pray. Hain't nuttin' gwanna he'p more den ta pray. But, Angel—" Harriet grasped the young woman's shoulders firmly between her strong hands—"de Lawd knows what's best. Jes' leabe et ta 'E. Dere's ben many's a time—at night—out in de da'k woods—listenin' ta de bayin' ob hounds huntin' fo' me an' dose what was wid me dat I knowd only de good Lawd stood atween weuns an' certain deat'.

Angel wiped her eyes. "I reckon' dat you es right, Harriet, but now I sho wisht dat I had come ta you fu'st 'bout Gilly."

"You done right, chil'," Harriet said. "What happened hain't none ob yo fault. An' Sam'l done right too." She hesitated, twisting her chin to one side to give Angel a quizzical look. "You know dat dat man lobes you, don' you, Angel?"

Angel stopped dead in her tracks. "Who? Samuel? You kyan't mean dat, Harriet!"

"Ob cawse 'e do. Et's written all obah 'e face ebery time dat 'e's neah you."

Angel could only stand there with her mouth hanging open. Surely Harriet couldn't be right. After Phoebe's death, Samuel had drawn inside of himself. Then, when he'd heard the calling, he'd thrown himself completely into the Lord's work.

"Eben a preacha' ob de Lawd es a man," Harriet said, as though she'd read Angel's innermost thoughts.

"But Phoebe—"

"Phoebe's ben dead a long time, gal. Et's you now dat Sam'l's got his eye 'pon."

"Bu—but what should I do?"

Harriet slapped her knee and laughed out loud. "Do, gal? Dere hain't a t'ing you kin do 'bout dat! Mens es funny dat-a-way. Effen dey set dere heart 'pon you, den de mo' you push 'em away, de mo' dey's gwanna want you!"

Thus it was that when Samuel came to pick up Angel later that afternoon, she suddenly felt terribly shy in his presence. He was so bubbling over with excitement that he barely noticed, but Angel had all she could do to hobble along beside him. Goodness, but he was a big man! And so strong! His face looked like it had been chiseled from black granite; still, there was a certain softness to it. And his eyes burned with intelligence. Stealing sideward glances, Angel felt as if her heart was fairly bursting out of her chest.

They reached the Oaks home when the last hot rays of the sun were lengthening the shadows of the trees on the lawn. The planter's mansion had, like many other homes in Beaufort, taken a rather bad beating, but it still spoke of opulence and grace. Angel waited on the front porch while Samuel went inside to speak quietly to one of the army medical officers standing in the hallway. There was a silence, then the shuffling of several feet.

When she turned toward Samuel's voice, she saw a young white man standing next to him. He was tall but terribly emaciated. His hair, a sandy brown gone prematurely gray at the temples, was slicked down to his head as though he had fingered water through it. His face was gaunt, even slightly wasted, but there was a brightness in his eyes that spoke of both humor and intelligence.

Samuel put his big hand on the young man's shoulder as he escorted him out through the doorway. Samuel's smile was so broad that it creased his entire face. His white teeth shone like pearls, and smile wrinkles pulled at the corners of his eyes.

The young white man walked straight up to Angel. He lifted her hand in his, then surprisingly, leaned down his head and kissed it.

"Dis," said Samuel, as though he were announcing the worship hour's first hymn, "es Corp'al Jonathan Franklin."

Angel stood there perplexed, unable to answer, unable to even comprehend what Samuel was saying.

Samuel laughed out loud. "Et's de shock," he said, speaking sideways to Jonathan. "She jes' don' know what ta say."

Jonathan smiled at Angel and took both of her hands in his. "I'm the Yankee who Laura May wrote you about," he said simply. Then he had to catch a firm hold of Angel's arms, for her knees were turning to water. "It's such a pleasure to meet you, my dear. And I have so much to thank you for."

Chapter 7

Believer I Know

(December 1863 to February 1864)

Zach had seen the look on Samuel's face when he and Angel were together. Samuel just couldn't keep his eyes off her, though surely he must have known that she was Zach's girl. The very thought of this made Zach bristle with anger, but what was he to do? He was not a free agent like Samuel. He couldn't simply walk away from his regiment at will just to go'a courting. Samuel, on the other hand, was able to be with Angel whenever he wished.

The problem made Zach toss and turn on his cot at night and kept him on edge through the long, tedious days of drilling and marching. Only when he was out on a foraging expedition or involved in one of the hit-and-run raids that his regiment was becoming noted for did he find relief from his worries.

Despite Angel's concerns, the trouble brewing over Cudjo's death didn't really worry Zach. After all, what could those government men prove? They didn't understand the first thing about voodoo and black magic. Everything to them must be cut and dried, cause and effect. Cudjo had died from uncontrollable fear when he realized that a spell had been placed on him, not from poison—or at least that's what Zach hoped was the case. At any rate, it was over and done with, and the sooner he put it out of his mind, the better.

Zach had tried to talk to Angel about his concerns over

Samuel's growing attentions, but every time they were together, which wasn't often, Angel seemed harried and overworked. She took her duties at the contraband hospital too seriously, as far as he was concerned. He couldn't imagine what all the fuss was about. Zach had heard of the newly formed "Invalid Corps" made up of disabled soldiers who were being put to work in the military hospitals. And goodness knows there were enough disabled soldiers around! Why women should be allowed in any army facility, even a hospital, during wartime was more than Zach could fathom. But Angel had met his efforts to convince her to return to Coosaw with little more than a stony glare. He'd even suggested that she stay on to help out at the school over on St. Helena. For this he had received an angry retort that left him smarting for days. What had gotten into this young woman he so loved? She was making a fool of herself hobbling around that contraband hospital as though her efforts were really needed!

But none of these feelings had advanced his cause with Angel. She gradually became more distant, even cold toward him. And he, in turn, began staying away from her for longer periods of time, hoping that the separation would do them both good. Perhaps Angel simply needed to learn to appreciate him more. Now if he could only think of something to do about Samuel, he might be able to relax for a while and let nature take its course. Angel was sure to tire of hospital work eventually. And once she got back to Coosaw, he could easily convince her that they should marry and start a family as soon as possible.

Of course, that didn't mean that he was going to give up the army. Army life suited him well. He actually found himself hoping that the war would last for a good long time so he could continue with what he loved to do best. He would see to it that he got home on leave often enough to keep Angel happy. But then, just as fast as possible, he would get back to his regiment. It was a near-perfect dream, but for some reason, one that Angel did not seem to share. And so, to lessen his anxiety, he volunteered for one dangerous raid after another.

In August, Zach joined an expedition that traveled up the Edisto River. The mission entailed blowing up a bridge on the Charleston and Savannah Railway. It was all part of the campaign to cut off supplies to Charleston, but in the end, it turned out to be a frustrating failure. The raiding party traveled upriver in three river steamers, but as small as the vessels were, they could barely negotiate the twists and turns of the upper Edisto. And to further complicate the situation, the Confederate defenders of the railway had sunk thick wooden pilings, fence-post fashion, across the riverbed at its most strategic points. The pilings proved to be a very effective deterrent.

Not more than a mile or two from the railway, the steamer on which Zach was traveling was disabled by the sunken pilings. Having lost its steerage, the vessel swirled helplessly in the current, then grounded itself on a partially exposed mud flat. Its would-be raiders, frustrated into silence, listened to the distant sounds of gunfire and knew that their cause was lost. One steamer had made it through, but it was taking a terrible pounding from the Rebel gun batteries that had been hidden on the banks of the river.

Zach stood on the open deck of the small river steamer and felt the heat of a merciless sun glaring down on him. It was like standing on an overheated griddle. By constantly shifting from one spot to another, he managed to keep his feet from blistering, but his discomfort was acute. Two men standing near him dropped from sunstroke, one of whom died later that day. To know that they were so close to their objective, yet so completely immobile, only added to their disappointment. And during all of this, the Rebel cavalry units rode triumphantly up and down the riverbanks, taking potshots at the exposed men on the small steamers.

Their escape was equally dishonorable. Desperate to get away without any further loss of life, Colonel Higginson ordered his men to move en masse, first to one side of the deck, then the other. Miraculously, they managed to rock the vessel just enough to loosen it from the mud flat. The outgoing tide did the rest. With their ammunition almost exhausted and their vessel's engine threatening to die at any moment, the ill-fated expedition descended the Edisto River having destroyed nothing. They did, however, manage to carry away a large number of refugee slaves from the nearby plantations, so all was not completely lost.

Just after Christmas, with the new year of 1864 promising to be as filled with adventure as the one before it, Zach set off on another scouting expedition, this time up the Combahee River. Once the raiding party reached the railroad, they set to work on the telegraph wires, cutting them in order to intercept and read the dispatches going back and forth between Charleston and Savannah. The whole affair was a source of great merriment for them, until some observant person on a passing train spotted the hanging wires. There followed yet another wild escape downriver, with Rebel cavalry troops in hot pursuit. But this time, things did not go quite as smoothly. Three of Zach's companions were captured, and several more were killed. Zach, as usual, came away without a scratch. He began to think of himself as exceptionally lucky, if not almost indestructible.

Thus it was that on his next trip into Beaufort, Zach decided it was high time to stop by the contraband hospital and visit Angel. Surely she must be missing him a great deal by now. And more than likely, the wounded men from the last raid had seen her and told her about his exploits. She'd be worried, of course, thinking that he was taking too many chances, pushing his luck a bit too far.

But when he entered the hospital house, he was surprised to learn that Angel already had a visitor, a white soldier known as Corporal Franklin. "Dey es out in de backyaad," said the medical orderly on duty at the front desk. "Las' I seen, dey was settin' under dat big oak tree near de back ob de prope'ty."

At first, Zach couldn't place the name. Corporal Franklin? Now, who was *he*? Ah yes, that Yankee prisoner fellow who, thanks to Laura May, had managed to escape from the Columbia stockade.

"What's 'e doin' he'e?" asked Zach brusquely, unable to keep the irritation out of his voice. He knew it was a foolish question. Of course, the corporal would have much to tell Angel about Laura May and the conditions in Columbia. Still, it annoyed him.

" 'E's one ob dem Invalid Corps peoples," sniffed the orderly, obviously disapproving of this new concept that might well put him out of a noncombat job.

After a short search, Zach found Angel and Jonathan sitting on a bench on the grounds behind the hospital. They were engaged in a deep conversation and hardly noticed his approach. For some strange reason, this, too, made Zach very angry.

Looking up with surprise and pleasure, Angel patted the bench and invited Zach to sit down next to her. He declined, preferring, rather, to remain standing with his back propped against the nearby oak.

Dis Jonathan fellow looks fit 'nuff ta me, thought Zach. *Why hain't 'e rejoined 'e old outfit?* Humph, the Invalid Corps indeed! It was just another excuse for staying out of the fighting.

As if she had read his mind, Angel explained that the rigors of a long captivity had played havoc with Jonathan's digestive system. He suffered from bloody discharges and repeated bouts of nausea and weakness. Still, while he was unfit for combat duty, Jonathan refused to return north to recuperate. Preferring to remain useful to the cause, he had chosen to stay on in Beaufort, where he could work at least part time in one of the military hospitals.

"When this war is over," Jonathan said earnestly, "I hope to go back to medical school. I only need another two years, and I'll be finished. My father's a doctor. He has a thriving medical practice in Philadelphia. He's got it all planned out that the two of us will go into partnership when I finish school."

Hesitating, Jonathan looked down at his hands. "I've thought about it a lot lately, but this war has made me see things in a completely different way. I'm afraid my father isn't going to understand this, but—well—I don't think I want to go back to Philadelphia. I kind of like it right here in Beaufort. It would be a nice place to settle down." He glanced at Angel, and a knowing look passed between them.

Zach only nodded. He wasn't much interested in Corporal Franklin's plans for the future. But the young invalid didn't seem to notice Zach's lack of enthusiasm. He went right on talking, taking up Zach's precious time when he and Angel could be alone.

"My dad went to Johns Hopkins—that's a university in Maryland. I went there, too, until this war started. I hope I'll be able to go back, but first I've got to be certain that Laura May is safe. I owe her a lot, you see. She's—well—she's very special to me."

Zach looked closely at Jonathan's face. So that was the lay of the land, was it? He was in love with Laura May. Yes, now he remembered that Angel had told him as much. Well, good for him. He hoped it would all work out for the two of them. But most of all, he wanted this talkative fellow to make himself scarce.

Sensing Zach's growing impatience, Angel tried to defuse the situation by changing the subject. "Zach, I es gwanna take a few days off ta go back ta Coosaw ta see Maum Beezie. Den mayhap I might could eben go obah ta St. Helena. We done heard dat Mizz Murry's been awful sick. I'd kinna like ta visit wid she."

Zach looked at her in confusion. He never could keep all of these northern missionaries straight. "Who's Mizz Murry?" he asked, his voice flat.

"Zach, sure 'nuff you mus' 'members Mizz Murry! Why, she's de teacher friend ob Mizz Laura Towne. Mizz Towne's ben nigh worried sick 'bout she. Eben stayed he'e fo' Christmas, 'stead ob goin' back No'th ta visit wid she fambly. De doctah say dat Mizz Murry come near ta dyin' wid de malaria feber, an' effen Mizz Towne hadn' done stayed, she sho' 'nuff would-a died!"

At this point, Jonathan stood up and excused himself. "I've got to get back to my duties, folks." He reached out to shake Zach's hand. "It's a pleasure meeting you, Zach. I'm sure you and Angel have a lot to talk about. Forgive me if I've interrupted your visit."

Then, reaching out again, Jonathan grasped Angel's hands

affectionately. "I'll send over those melons first thing in the morning," he said. "I'm sorry that you people are having such difficulties getting provisions and such. It all seems terribly unfair, doesn't it!"

Angel thanked him, then kept her eyes on his retreating back. She seemed reluctant to have Jonathan leave, or was it, wondered Zach, that she would just rather not be alone with him?

"What 'e mean 'bout not habin' perwisions?" he asked.

Angel sighed and turned to face Zach. "De white hospitals hab lots ob peoples ta sponsor dem, Zach—send dem food an' bandages an' such like. We don' get near 'nuff ob what we needs he'e."

"An' why's dat?" Zach asked.

Angel just shrugged. "Dat's jes' de way et be," she answered quietly.

"Jes' de way et be? Ha! Well, den et's 'bout time fo' et ta change!" Zach's voice rose with anger.

"Zach." Angel grasped his arm firmly. "You es a brave man, I knows dat. An' I knows dat dere's been many a times dat you done what you taught was right fo' ta he'p me. I 'preciate et, Zach, I surely do. Bu—but sometimes you jes' try too hard. You kyan't change de wuld all by youse'f! An' what's de point ob et all anysomehow—fo' you an' me, I mean—effen in de end you jes' get youse'f kilt? What good es dat gwanna do us, Zach? Jes' tell me dat."

"I hain't no braver den de next man, Angel," Zach said vehemently. "But someplace 'long de way, I gotsta be mah own pusson. De buckra what comes down he'e, dey all talk mighty big 'bout how dey es he'pin' we po' colo'd folks. But when dey look at me, Angel, dey don' see no man. Dey don' eben see a so'dier. All dey see es anuder po' niggra what dey's gotsta look out fo'."

Angel was perplexed. "But Zach, I taught you say dat you liked de a'my 'cause et made you feel like you was doin' sumpin' impo'tant. Hain't dat 'nuff fo' now?"

Zach nodded. "I do likes de a'my. Cunnel Higginson, 'e say dat I es gwanna be a sa'geant soon de way I es goin', an' dat's what I wants most ob all." There was a sudden flash of enthusiasm in Zach's face, which just as quickly vanished. "But I tells you dis, gal, I seen some t'ings dat makes me mo' fightin' mad den eben de Seceshes do. We got a black sa'geant now what's de bestest young offisuh in de whole regiment. Dat man, 'e coulda ben a gen'l effen 'e got half de chance. But seein' as how 'e was nebah 'lowed ta get no ed-ecation, 'e hain't nebah gwanna be no mo' den a plain sa'geant!"

"Zach, dere hain't no point in—"

"Don' go unrablin' yo mout', 'omans, befo' I finish talkin'! Dis es sumpin' I gotsta say." Zach pounded his fist against his hand for emphasis. "Dese young buckra boys what don' know de fust t'ing 'bout bein a so'dier, dey come down he'e wid brass all obah dey shoulde's an' stripes all up an' down dey a'ms. Tellin' weuns what ta do an' jes' how ta do et. Now dey tellin' us dat we es only gwanna get half ob de pay what de white so'diers gets. Hah! De fact es, we hain't seen eben dat much yet. Effen we gets seben dolla's, Angel, t'ree ob dats gotta go fo' ta pay fo' dis unifo'm." Zach pulled roughly at his jacket as he talked. "De res', et all goes fo' our food an' guns. Et hain't right, Angel. Et jes' hain't right!"

Angel lowered her face and sighed. "I know dat, Zach," she answered. "I know et hain't right." She sighed deeply again. "De same t'ings happin' he'e in dis colo'd hospital. Kyan't hardly find no doctahs ta come he'e an' takes care ob dese po' boys what's sick an' wounded. No med'cines half de time. An' food? Huh, weuns es al'ys scroungin' round jes' ta fin' sumpin' ta feed 'em wid. Salt po'k an' co'n meal, dat's all dey gib we. How kin a man what's near bled ta deat' gets betta on jes' salt po'k an' a mess ob weavily co'n meal?"

Suddenly exhausted and discouraged by this sharing of their frustrations, Angel and Zach sat quietly looking into their hands. Finally, Zach turned and grasped Angel's shoulders. "I guess none ob et makes much sense, do et? But leastways, we got each uddah. An' I do lobes you, Angel honey! Honest I do!"

She leaned her head on his shoulder and felt the warmth and strength of his arms as they encircled her. How she had longed for this, to hear him say these words, to feel the gentleness that she always knew he was capable of. And he was right. They could make things work out somehow. The unfairness of the world that they faced could be managed as long as they had each other.

Renewed with hope, they held onto each other and let this new closeness wash away their pain. The shadows of the overhanging oak branches lengthened and the air grew colder, but they hardly noticed. Finally, Zach pulled himself away. Holding Angel at arms' length, he smiled down at her with a look of possession in his eyes.

"Den et's all settled, hain't et!" he said emphatically.

Angel felt suddenly perplexed. "What's all settled, Zach?"

"Why, you an' me, Angel honey. Now you kin stop all ob dis foolish nursin' stuff an' go on back ta Coosaw. 'Course, we es gwanna hafta hold off some afo' we jump de broomstick tugedda, but I figure dat you won' mind waitin'." Zach stood up to his full height. Looking every bit the soldier that he was, he thrust back his shoulders and tucked his chin tightly down against his neck.

Angel felt confused. What did he mean by saying that she'd give up her nursing career? Surely he wasn't going back to that old tune! Hadn't he heard what she had told him time and time again?

Unaware of Angel's confusion and rapidly changing mood, Zach went on to describe how she could wait for him on Coosaw while he and his regiment went off to fight in a battle that was going on in Florida. Only this time, he explained, she'd have to be very patient, for it wouldn't be a quick affair. The whole regiment was packing up. They were to desert Camp Shaw by the end of the week and turn it over to a fresh regiment coming down from Maine. In fact, they'd already received their marching orders. It was obvious to Angel that Zach could hardly wait to be underway.

Trying desperately to recapture what they had had just moments before, Angel stood up and reached out to Zach. She pressed her fingers against his lips. "Hush!" she said, her voice breaking with tears. "Jes' hush up, Zach!" The tears began spilling down her cheeks, but she didn't care. Let him see her cry. What he was doing to her was cruel and almost too painful for words.

Now it was Zach's turn to be puzzled. "What you cryin' fo', gal?" he asked. "I done said we was gwanna jump de broomstick. Hain't dat what you al'ys wanted?"

"When?" asked Angel. "Afta you come back from annuda battle? Afta you gets you legs shot off or—or lose you a'm? You 'spect me ta do nuttin' all dat time but sit dere 'pon Coosaw jes' worryin' an' wond'rin' effen you es still alibe or dead?"

"But, Angel, you jes' said dat dis he'e hospital place hain't doin' nuttin' but makin' you fret. No doctahs, you say! No med'cine! No food! So dere's no use stayin' he'e effen you hain't got nuttin ta wu'k wid."

He grabbed her shoulders and shook her gently as though to force some sense into her head. "What you gwanna learn he'e dat you kyan't learn 'pon Coosaw, gal? You already knows how ta clean out slop buckets an' mop de flo'. Dis hain't no place fo' you, Angel! Et hain't no place fo' de gal what's gwanna marry me!"

Angel set her jaw tight and pushed him away. "You es 'bout as orn'ry as a mule, Zach, an' sometime jes' as mean. I hain't leabin' dis hospital, not jes' yet. Mayhap effen et was like et uset ta be—befo' dey let de colo'd mens go off ta be so'diers, den mayhap I could ob jes' stayed on at Coosaw an' ben de same kinda nurse what Maum Beezie was. But dis wah, et's changed eberyt'ing. I gotsta do what I can fo' mah own people, jes' like you gotsta do what you es doin'."

Zach's face grew cold and hard. He stretched himself up tall and blew out a long puff of air. "Well, den, I guess et's settled fo' de time bein'," he said. His voice had a strange edge to it. He turned and started to walk away, but then stopped and looked back at Angel. Pressing his lips tightly together, he tipped his head to one side and looked at her earnestly as though to say that he was giving her one last chance.

Angel could feel herself trembling, but the tears were gone now.

The afternoon had suddenly grown fiercely cold. There was a ringing in her ears, as though some inner voice were trying to get through to her conscious mind but couldn't quite make it.

Zach waited stoically for her reply, but when none came, he turned his mouth into an angry snarl. "An' Sam'l?" he asked. "What's gwanna happin now wid you an' Sam'l?"

"What's dat mean, Zach?"

"You knows 'zactly what I mean, Angel. 'E's sweet on you, hain't 'e!"

"Zach! Sam'l's a friend—jes' a good friend. Why, you knows dat."

"Uh-huh, I knows dat, but et hain't de way Sam'l sees et! Sam'l's sweet on you, Angel. I ben knowin' dat fo' a long time. An' 'e's done figu'd dat 'e's gwanna make you his gal. Now tell me de trut', Angel; es dat what you wan'? 'Cause effen et is, den I hain't got no place aside you."

Angel was so stunned that she could only shake her head. It was as though she had suddenly lost her power of speech.

Zach waited not a second longer. Turning on his heels, he spun around and walked quickly away. Once, just before he rounded the corner of the house, Angel almost called out to him. But somehow, she couldn't. She felt weak and powerless, all of her senses reeling into some great black void.

Some minutes later, when the darkness of the coming night began to creep into her very bones, Angel slumped down onto the cold bench. "Yes, Zach!" she whispered. "I lobes you. I really do lobes you!"

But he was gone, and there was nothing left to do but turn and go back into the hospital. As Angel mounted the last step and entered the doorway, Harriet Tubman moved out of the shadows. "Et's ha'd sometimes, chil'," she said, "ta be eberyt'ing ta all de folks what needs you. I knows! Beliebe me, I knows!" She hugged Angel close, cradling her head like a mother comforting a frightened child. "An' sometimes," she said in a whisper, "de hardest kind ob lobe es de lettin' go kind."

Chapter 8

On Sweet St. Helena Isle

(February 1864)

Angel's trip back to Coosaw was a dark blur, so despondent was she over her falling out with Zach. She alternately felt angry and remorseful, betrayed and guilty. If only she had tried to placate Zach's feelings. But would that have been honest? No, she didn't think so.

Then, to make matters worse, it was Samuel who had carried her back to the island in his small boat. She had spoken hardly a word to him all the way. Poor man, she thought, he really wasn't to blame for all this mess. Or was he?

Zach had been right; Angel saw that now. Samuel's eyes literally shone every time he looked at her. There was no doubt that he was in love with her. No, more than that, he was downright stricken. He hung onto her every word as though it were a pronouncement from above. He went to excessive lengths to make her comfortable. Was the sun too hot? He'd put up the extra sail as an awning. Was the current too rough? He'd move closer in toward the shallows. Was she hungry? Was she tired? And on and on.

None of this really registered until they were within sight of Coosaw's docks. Then she had an overwhelming urge to simply dive into the water and swim the rest of the way to shore. It was, of course, a foolish thought. She'd never learned how to swim. But right now, she desperately needed to be free from

Samuel's smothering attention.

When she and Maum Beezie were finally alone, Angel breathed a sigh of relief. Thankfully, her grandmother had done quite well in her absence. The women of the quarters, loving the old matriarch as deeply as Angel did, had taken turns caring for her. Angel could see that she wanted for little.

The rheumatism in Maum Beezie's legs had left her permanently crippled, but some kindhearted Yankee officer had sent over to one of the hospitals and gotten an old wooden wheelchair for her. Each morning she would be wheeled to her doorstep, where she could spend an hour or two watching the activities in the yard. Or if she chose, she could simply doze in the sun.

That first evening was an important one for Angel. She desperately needed to unburden herself. She and Maum Beezie stayed up for hours talking. Or rather, Angel talked while Maum Beezie listened attentively.

She told her grandmother everything. How Zach had stayed away for weeks on end. How he had thrown himself into the most dangerous assignments. How she had worried over his apparent disinterest, then been raised to near ecstasy by his declaration of love. Finally, she told Maum Beezie that Zach fully expected her to give up her nursing while he went gallivanting off with the army. " 'E says dat I should jes' come back ta Coosaw an' wait fo' 'e," she said, lines of anger pulling down the corners of her mouth. " 'E says dat I might jes' as well, seein's how I hain't doin' nuttin' impo'tant at de hospital."

Maum Beezie could see the pain in her granddaughter's eyes and understood how deeply that remark must have hurt her. She clicked her tongue and shook her head sadly, but still, she said nothing. Sitting on the floor, her shoulders slumped, a look of dejection on her face, Angel watched the long tongues of orange flame lick hungrily at the pine logs that Samuel had brought in earlier. She felt exhausted but knew that there was no sleep in her. The old feelings of guilt were resurfacing. *Perhaps*, she thought, *I'es makin' dis soun' too one-sided.* She knew that Maum Beezie was a stickler for looking at all sides of an issue. Perhaps that's why she was saying nothing—giving no advice.

"Maum Beezie—" Angel hesitated, finding this next bit hard to say. "Zach, 'e say dat Sam'l es sweet on me." There was another long silence. " 'E say dat—well—'e say dat dat's why 'e's been stayin' away."

Maum Beezie nodded. "Mm-hm," she answered, "I done 'spected dat, honey lamb."

"But—but what should I do, den?"

"KI, CHIL'!" Maum Beezie fairly chuckled her reply. "Hain't nuttin' you kin do 'bout dat!"

Angel was stunned. She expected advice, not laughter. Surely Maum Beezie was not insensitive to the seriousness of this matter!

Angel opened her mouth to protest, but her grandmother held up her hand. "All in de good Lawd's time, chil'. You wait an' see; et'll come out de way et's meant ta be. Hain't I tol' you a hun'red times dat Gawd al'ys knows what's best fo' weuns?"

Angel pressed the tips of her fingers against her forehead and sighed. " 'Course I 'members what you said, but dis he'e es dif'ent. Hain't you al'ays tol' me dat de Lawd, 'E had a pu'pose fo' mah life?"

Maum Beezie smiled and nodded her agreement.

"Well, when I seen all de misery an' trouble dat dis wah es bringin', I knowed right away what dat pu'pose was. I es sp'osed ta be in dat hospital, Gramma. I hain't sp'osed ta be jes' sittin' he'e while all de uddah peoples wuks an' sac'fices 'emselbes!"

"Who is all dem uddah peoples you es talkin' 'bout, Angel?"

"Why, all kinds ob peoples, Gramma. Mizz Towne and Mizz Murry, dey left eberyt'ing ahind 'em an' come down he'e fo' ta he'ps we. An' Mizz Tubman—hain't nobody what does fo' she own like-a dat 'omans do. An' den dere's Mizz Clara Barton. Why, dat 'oman's a saint fo' sho'! An' effen I could do jes' half ob what—"

Maum Beezie shook her head and reached out to touch Angel's shoulder. "Chil'! Chil'!" she said. "Don' you knows what kinda price dem 'omans gotsta pay fo' all dat good wuk? None ob dem hab a man fo' ta lobes 'em or takes care ob 'em. An' none ob 'em, mo' den likely, es eber gwanna hab any chilluns or raise dere own famblies. Es dat what you wants?"

Angel dropped her head and pressed her clenched fists into her lap. "No," she answered, her voice sounding very distant. She lifted her face and looked into her grandmother's eyes. "But—but I taught dat mayhap, jes' mayhap, I kin hab all two." There was a look of pleading in her eyes now.

"Hab all two ob what, chil'?"

"You know, Maum Beezie, mah nursin' *an'* mah own fambly."

The elderly woman sighed deeply. Her voice sounded tired and uncertain when she spoke. "Mayhap," she said. Then she turned and faced Angel squarely. Her blurred, old eyes seemed suddenly very clear and well focused. "But den, honey lamb," she said quietly, "you es gwanna hafta find somebody asides Zach. You es gwanna hafta find somebody what wants de same t'ings what you wants."

Angel caught her breath. When she finally spoke, there were tears in her voice. "Maum Beezie, you don' t'ink dat Zach es de right man fo' me, does you?"

The old woman didn't answer right away. She had a faraway look in her eyes, as though she were seeing something painful that had happened a long time ago. Finally, she reached out her gnarled hand and laid it gently on Angel's knee.

"You knows dat li'l ol' peach tree out in de corner ob mah yaad—de one dat's close ta dem big pines?" she asked.

Angel nodded, wondering what that poor, overshadowed tree had to with her relationship with Zach.

"Ol' Massa Weldon—de one befo' Gilly's an' Laura May's papa—'e uset ta lobe mah peach pies," Maum Beezie said, settling back in her chair as she recalled old memories. " 'E uset ta say dat I could bake a betta peach pie den anysomebody 'e eber did know. Den one day, 'e come ridin' up carryin' dis li'l ol' peach tree ahind 'e. Said dat she'd ben growin' out in de field by de Big House. Said dat de uddah peach trees 'round she—de big ones—dey was growin' de bestest peaches in de whole Sou!"

She paused, her eyes twinkling as she thought of the power

her cooking had had on the old master. " 'E say dat 'e wants ta gib me dis li'l tree ta grow in mah own yaad, so's when de peaches come, dey be right dere, close by."

Maum Beezie was silent for a moment; then her voice grew low and very serious. "De ol' massa, 'e done pulled dat po' li'l ol' tree right up by she roots. Stick she in de groun' in de wu'stest place dere was. Dem big ol' loblolly pines all 'round she—cuttin' out de sun—takin' de sweetness from de eart' under she roots!"

Angel shuddered, for there was an anger in her grandmother's voice that she'd seldom heard before. "Maum Beezie," she said, "hain't no point in bringin' up ol'—"

"You lets me finish dis, chil'. Et's sumpin' you gotsta know." She swallowed hard, then continued. "Ol' Massa Weldon, what 'e done, et weren't right. Dat was greed what made 'em yank up dat li'l tree, an' et be greed what was de ruin ob she."

Angel was beginning to understand. "Dat tree neber did grow no peaches, did she, Gramma?"

"Um-mm," answered the old woman, shaking her head sadly. "Not ta speak ob. Oh, once er twice, she had some po' li'l t'ings what jes' shribeled up befo' dey dropped off. An' I tried mah best, sho nuff I did! I watahed an' gentled she 'long fo' years, but de damage already bin done."

Maum Beezie fell quiet again as she thought of the long, hard years when the master of the land had damaged far more than just her tree. Finally, she smiled down at Angel. "But de pines an' de oaks, dey do jes' fine in mah yaad! Come sto'ms, dey bend an' sometimes break. But befo' you know et, chil', dey's holdin' up dere arms ta de sun jes' like al'ys. Den de sun, she grows too hot, an' de draught come. Dem pines an' oaks, dey jes' hold what li'l watah dey kin get and keep on growin'."

Angel smiled, thinking of the life-giving beauty of the great pines and oaks that surrounded Maum Beezie's cabin.

"Angel honey," said the old woman, "I al'ys taught dat you was sumpin' like dem oaks an' pines. No mattah what happens, you es gwanna find some way ta manage."

She hesitated, as though what she had to say next was very painful. When she did speak, it was quietly. "Zach, 'e's sumpin' like dat po' li'l peach tree. Now 'e hain't stunted none ta look at, mind you, but dere es sumpin' what happened ta 'e when dey pulled 'e up from de ground 'e be growin' in. Et's like a part ob 'e got bad marred when 'e was yanked up by de roots."

She sighed heavily, burdened by the terrible things that had happened to so many of her people. "An' now dat 'e's a man," she continued, " 'e hain't neber gwanna fo'get dat sumpin' impo'tant was takin' away when 'e was too small ta fight back. Dat's why 'e's fightin' so hard now, Angel. An' dat's why 'e's gwanna hold onto what 'e t'inks es his. He's gwanna hold on so tight dat 'e'll choke de life right out ob she!"

Angel shuddered. Yes, Maum Beezie was right. Zach's love for army life, his efforts to seek out the most dangerous assignments, his possessive ways, his obstinate refusal to even consider her needs—it was all a part of this thing that was tearing them apart. And she couldn't change him any more than he could change her.

That night, Angel lay in her bed and tried to think of what she should do. By morning, she was more exhausted than rested. And she could see that the late hours had also taken a heavy toll on her grandmother. Zach would soon be leaving with his regiment to go to Florida. There was no point in going back to Beaufort to try to talk with him; he'd be far too busy. Besides, what would she say? No, as usual, Maum Beezie was right. This was something quite beyond her capabilities. She would have to leave it in the Lord's hands and trust that no matter what happened, it would be for the best.

Angel stayed with her grandmother for most of that week. She caught up on the cleaning and sewing, worked in the garden, and made tasty meals that put smiles on her grandmother's face and meat on her old bones. She visited with the other women in the quarters and invited them in for afternoon tea. Anything to keep busy! Anything to keep from thinking about Zach!

Finally, one late afternoon, Maum Beezie called to her. She thanked Angel for all that she had done but reminded her that a visit to Miss Towne and Miss Murry was long overdue. "Dem 'oomans hab bin mighty kind ta you, Angel, an' I done heard dat dere's some trouble fo' 'em."

"What kind ob trouble, Maum Beezie?" Angel asked.

"Dere's some what say dat dey kyan't use de brick chu'ch no mo' fo' ta habe dey school. An' dey es sp'osed ta move out ob de Oaks house an' go ta some po' li'l place up in Saint Hel'nasville."

Angel was startled by this news. What would happen to the school if there were no longer a building available for its use? And she knew what sort of decrepit, old homes—just cottages, really—stood over in Saint Helenasville. Why, on that exposed piece of land, the ocean-born winds would blow right through the walls! And Miss Murry had been so terribly sick! Angel had heard that the poor woman had no other family to go to. She had planned on making these islands and their people her life's work.

Yes, Angel must go to them as soon as possible. There was little she could do to influence the authorities on their behalf, and even less that she could give them in the way of material things, but she could show them that she cared. And she *could* give them her support. The Gullah people of the islands must rally to the women's cause. It would only take a few words spoken at the right time to galvanize them into action; the people loved their missionary teachers, who had come to help them help themselves. Once again, it was Samuel who took her over to Saint Helena Island. He seemed terribly subdued this time, as though he carried a great burden of worry. The sparkle was gone from his eyes, and he seemed distracted, almost nervous.

Oh no! thought Angel. Perhaps Zach had said something to Samuel, after all. Perhaps he'd even threatened him. Angel wouldn't put it past Zach; he was obviously very jealous of her affections.

Still, Samuel did not seem to want to talk of his troubles, so Angel decided not to press him. He brought her to the landing point and arranged for an oxcart to take her the rest of the way to what had once been the Oaks Plantation. It was a lovely day. A gentle breeze rustled the evergreen leaves of the oaks and the dried fronds of the palmettos. The oyster shell roadway sparkled in the warm sunlight.

They approached the brick church nestled in its sheltering oak grove just as the school's opening exercises were beginning. On such a lovely day, it was common for the teachers to lead their young charges outside to sit in the soft grass beneath the overhanging trees. Angel could see a veritable cloud of small, dark heads. Then the sound of children's singing came to her, the sweet voices piping and chirping in time with the happy rhythm of the morning's hymn. Ah yes, she knew that song well!

> Oh, none in all the world before
> Were ever glad as we!
> We're free on Carolina's shore,
> We're all at home and free.

Motioning for the driver of the cart to stop so she could better hear the words, Angel began singing along with the children.

> Thou Friend and Helper of the poor,
> Who suffered for our sake,
> To open every prison door,
> And every yoke to break!
>
> Bend low Thy pitying face and mild,
> And help us sing and pray;
> The hand that blessed the little child,
> Upon our foreheads lay.

Suddenly, the overhanging trees were filled with bird song, making the lovely hymn all the more beautiful. It was as though even the little creatures of the island had joined their voices in praise to God, their source of freedom.

> We hear no more the driver's horn,
> No more the whip we fear,

> This holy day that saw Thee born
> Was never half so dear.
>
> The very oaks are greener clad,
> The waters brighter smile;
> Oh, never shone a day so glad
> On sweet St. Helena's Isle.
>
> We praise Thee in our songs today,
> To Thee in prayer we call,
> Make swift the feet and straight the way
> Of freedom unto all.

Tears filled Angel's eyes. Her throat felt choked and restricted. She could no longer sing, but the voices of the children continued. They had come to the last, triumphant verse, and now even the massive oaks seemed to vibrate with the power of the words.

> Come once again, O blessed Lord!
> Come walking on the sea!
> And let the mainlands hear the word
> That sets the island free!*

Remembering that bright Christmas Day just a little over two years ago—remembering how, as grown as she was, she had stood with the children of the Sea Islands and sung this same hymn, Angel's heart soared. Yes, she had made the right decision, she knew that now. She loved Zach with all her heart, but she loved these people too. She loved them so much that she could not sacrifice their needs, or her own, for that matter, to Zach's restricted visions. And perhaps, in time, he, too, would come around. There was hope, she knew. There was always hope!

The driver took her right up to the front of the church and then helped her down. Miss Forten, the black teacher who had come from the North to teach at the school, was just stepping out of the doorway. She smiled and raised her hand to greet Angel, then, having much to do, hurried off to join her class. "On such a fine day," she called over her shoulder, her voice sounding very northern, very cultured, "we thought it would be nice to hold all of our classes out in the open."

Angel had it on the tip of her tongue to ask if they were indeed being put out of the church, but then she thought better of it. This dignified black woman had enough on her mind without having to satisfy Angel's curiosity.

Angel sat quietly in the shade of one of the oaks and listened as the lessons were being "spelled out." This rote activity, which included everyone simultaneously, the children especially loved. They smiled and clapped their hands in time with the words. Turning everything into song was a large part of their cultural heritage.

When afternoon finally came to an end and Angel was sitting on the porch of the Oaks house enjoying a cool lemonade with the three teachers, she saw Samuel coming up the road. He had that same hangdog look that she'd noticed earlier in the day, but now there was an added despondency to it. Thinking that Samuel must still be smarting over some insult from Zach, Angel felt a little stab of anger. Why must he come here now and spoil her day? Why must he give her those looks of virtuous suffering and unrequited adoration? Then she saw Samuel's eyes, and her heart gave a jolt.

"Angel," he said quietly, "I needs ta talk ta you a minute 'bout sumpin' bery impo'tant." The glance that he gave the other women on the porch spoke eloquently of his need to be alone with Angel. Nodding to him, the three teachers stood up and walked quietly into the house. Angel felt a shiver of apprehension go through her. Something was wrong; she could see it in his face. Could something have happened to Maum Beezie? *Oh, Gawd*, she prayed silently, *don' let anyt'ing happen now. I still need dat 'omans so much!*

Samuel stepped up onto the porch. His tall frame was bent; his face was gray and haggard. He looked as though he had aged ten years. Sitting down heavily on one of the rockers,

Samuel clenched his hands and pressed them into his lap.

Angel could feel her chin begin to quiver. She opened her mouth to say something, but nothing came out.

"Angel honey—" Samuel began, his voice choked and thin. He lifted his head and turned around to face her.

"Wha—what be wrong, Sam'l? Es et Maum Beezie?"

Samuel shook his head. Involuntarily, Angel let out a loud sigh of relief.

Samuel began again, obviously struggling over his words. "You knows dat de Fust Souf Ca'lina Reg'ment was goin' ta Flo'da," he said, his voice cracking. "You knows dat dey was s'posd' ta fight in dat battle oba near Jacksonbille, enty?"

Angel nodded. She could feel the beginnings of a sharp pain against the sides of her chest. "Et's Zach, den," she said quietly. " 'E's bin kilt!" A sob escaped her half-open lips.

"No," answered Samuel. " 'E hain't bin kilt. 'E hain't neber eben gone ta Flo'da. None ob de reg'ment hab gone."

"What den?" Angel was more than puzzled. What was Samuel talking about? What was he trying to tell her?

Samuel stood up and walked to the edge of the porch. He stood there for a while, looking out at the lengthening shadows. Then, slowly, he turned and faced Angel once more. There were tears in the corners of his eyes and a sheen of moisture on his upper lip. He reached up and wiped it away with the back of his sleeve. "De whole reg'ment, dey was all packed up an' on de ship ready ta go," he said, his voice sounding forced now, and a bit too firm. "But den sumpin' happen, an' dey had ta go back ta Camp Shaw."

Trying to understand what this man was saying, Angel shook her head and lifted her eyebrows. She could see that Samuel's hands were trembling. There was a grayness around his lips. "What, Sam'l? Please! Tell me what be wrong!"

"Et's de smallpox, Mizz Angel. Dere's bin a bad outbreak ob de smallpox."

SMALLPOX! The very name sent shivers of blinding fear through Angel's head. Nothing was more dreaded than this! There had been outbreaks of the disease that had wiped out whole companies—decimated whole regiments! And though there had been attempts to inoculate the combat troops against the deadly virus, there was never enough vaccine to go around, and even fewer physicians who knew how to properly administer it. And for the black troops, it was easy to conclude that they would be the very last to get the life-saving vaccine.

"Zach?" she asked, her voice sounding distant inside her head.

Samuel nodded.

"Bad?" she asked.

Again Samuel nodded. "Bery bad, Angel. " 'E's bery bad, fo' true!"

"Den we uns gotsta go right now, Sam'l. Weuns gotsta go an' see 'e!"

Samuel shook his head sadly. "Dey hain't gwanna let you see 'e, Angel."

"Bu-but why? He hain't already daid, es 'e?" Angel felt as though her legs would no longer support her. She reached out and grasped frantically at the porch railing.

"No," answered Samuel. "Zach, 'e's still alibe, but dey hain't gwanna let you see 'e. Dey done put 'e in de smallpox hospital—an'-an' 'e's done ben qua'ntined."

Quarantined! But surely they would let *her* see Zach! She was a nurse, wasn't she? She could stay there and take care of him, bathe away his fever, nurse him back to health. And then he would know—oh yes, that must be it—then he would know how important her skills really were!

---

* "Saint Helena Hymn was written by John Greenleaf Whittier upon the request of Charlotte Forten, first black instructor at Penn School. It was first sung on the island at Brick Baptist Church on Christmas Day 1862" (Ronald Daise, *Reminiscences of Sea Island Heritage* [Orangeburg, S.C.: Sandlapper Publishing, 1986], 105-111).

Chapter 9

Goodbye, Brudder;
Now God Bless You

(February 1864)

Angel stood near the tall iron gates and stared in at the armed guard who paced back and forth as though protecting a military command post or a cache of armaments. The somber house stood isolated and forbidding within the walled yard. Even today, with spring bearing down on the land and the air drenched with the smell of it, the house seemed gripped by an inner darkness.

Beyond the house, rising just above its green copper roof, was a column of thick smoke. Angel had been watching it for hours, and during all that time, the color and texture of it had changed little. Only its smell had been altered. At first, it had had the distinct stench of burning wool. But as the day progressed, a far more nauseating odor was noticeable. Angel's mind rebelled at thoughts of what it might be.

The contrast of the spring day and the dark, walled-up house had been made all the more obvious during the early afternoon. To the north of the house, an open field had at some time in the past been planted with daffodils and jonquils. Having gone wild, they spilled in a glorious profusion well beyond the broken fencing. Children, their laughter sounding bright and joyous, had come to gather the flowers. Above their heads, wispy nag's tail clouds swept across the bright blue dome of the sky.

All of this beauty had been lost on Angel, for before her stood the house now being used as a smallpox hospital. Within it was Zach. She had pleaded and cajoled the authorities responsible for medical security to allow her entrance, but to no avail. They had been very emphatic about the rules. The sign on the gate that read **QUARANTINED—NO ADMITTANCE** meant exactly that, they said.

And so she had stood there for hours on end, watching in the middle distance the steady plodding of the guard. Scrutinizing with a heavy heart the dark column of smoke. The guard had looked at her sympathetically once or twice but had said nothing. If it had stood on the moon, the house would not have been less accessible to her.

Samuel came with Angel in the morning and stayed as long as he could. But there were many pressing duties to be done. Indeed, his continued presence only seemed to aggravate her. Samuel finally took leave just before noon, promising Angel that he would be back shortly with some lunch. But when he did return, she merely waved him away.

About two in the afternoon, a contingent of groaning wagons came up the secluded road. The first one was piled high with what appeared to be fresh bedding. That was understandable, Angel thought, for they were obviously doing no laundry in that hospital. After its use, every piece of bedding was burned—thus the constant column of smoke.

Angel could see that the second wagon held provisions of food and possibly medicines. Riding on the jolting buckboard with the driver was a gray-haired man who must have, at one time, looked very distinguished. He had a finely shaped head and a wavy shock of brown hair that had gone gray at the temples. Now, however, he looked only haggard and bone weary.

A doctor, thought Angel. Poor man! What must it be like to watch young men die by the thousands? And the victims of this smallpox plague, did they reach out to him with shaking hands, pleading for a deliverance that he could not give?

When the wagon stopped at the gate for proper clearance, Angel stepped forward. "Please, Massa," she said, using the title of deference as naturally as though she were still a slave.

"I gots somebody in dere what I cares a pow'ful lot 'bout. Please, suh, could you bring me some word ob 'e?"

The physician looked down at Angel through bloodshot eyes. "What's his name, girl?"

"Zach, suh. Jes' Zach."

Looking exasperated, the doctor shook his head. "Could be half a dozen Zachs in there," he said. "Is he a nigger?"

Angel nodded. "Yes, suh. 'E's Co'pul Zach wid de Fust Ca'lina Reg'ment. You kyan't miss 'e. 'E's bery tall, Massa—an'-an' bery good lookin'!"

"Good looking?" The doctor let out a short laugh that sounded almost scornful. "Nobody with smallpox is good looking, girl!"

Shocked by the doctor's apparently cruel indifference, Angel stumbled backward. The gate swung open, and the wagons rumbled on up the oyster shell drive. Angel felt a cold pain in her chest. It swelled outward, numbing first her arms, then traveling in waves down her legs. She slumped to the ground, her hands pressed to her face, and began rocking back and forth. Samuel found her that way when he came back in the late afternoon.

He lifted her up in his strong arms and carried her over to the oxcart, which he had borrowed from a sympathetic friend. "Dis es jes' about 'nuff, Angel honey," he said firmly. "I es takin' you back home."

Angel protested weakly, but Samuel paid her no mind. He wrapped her in a warm blanket, then let her slump against his side as he cracked his whip and called out to the bony ox. When they were well on their way down the darkening roadway, he slipped his right arm around Angel and pulled her head against his chest.

Before sunup the next morning, Angel and Samuel were back at the gate of the smallpox hospital. Harriet Tubman had also come along, insisting that on this day Angel might need all the support she could get. Harriet had thought to bring along two folding chairs and several warm blankets, for the day was much cooler than yesterday, and there was the threat of rain.

Now the three of them waited and stared at the house. They

looked for all the world like a group of mourners at a sitting-up service. Finally, Samuel stirred himself. "Et's gettin' colder, Harriet," he said. "Wrap dat li'l gal in de blanket; den I es gwanna get sumpin' hot fo' weuns ta drink."

Samuel cleared a spot of ground, then went in search of kindling. Before long, he had a small fire going. Pulling a battered tin pot from the back of the cart, he boiled some water, then sprinkled in the dried leaves of a herb tea that Maum Beezie had given him. He poured a cup for Angel, but once again, she only waved it away.

"Angel honey," Samuel said, "I hain't gwanna let you get de chills, 'cause den you be de one what we es gwanna hafta set around an' pray fo'." Without another word, he reached out and grasped both of Angel's hands in his. Harriet picked up the cup of medicinal tea and in her most motherly manner started to spoon-feed the grieving girl.

The day grew steadily more dismal and overcast. By some time in midafternoon, the doctor again appeared at the door of the hospital house. An orderly led a sad-looking, sway-backed horse out of a side shed and helped the physician mount. Moving slowly down the drive, the horse and rider approached the gate and the waiting sentry.

Angel lifted her head, her eyes filled with pleading tears. Sighing deeply, the tired doctor dismounted as the guard locked the gate behind him. He stood over Angel, looking down at her with a mournful expression. Then, wiping the weariness from his eyes with the flat of his hand and letting out another long sigh, he began to speak. "It was a fellow by the name of Zach that you were asking for, wasn't it?"

Angel nodded. Frightened at what was surely coming, Samuel and Harriet pressed close to their young friend.

"Well, then," said the doctor, "I'm sorry to tell you this, but I'm afraid he's dead."

The silence that followed was almost as frightening as the look on Angel's face. Then suddenly, she bent forward. A low, keening sound escaped her lips. Samuel reached for her, certain that she was going to fall, but Angel jerked away from him with such force that he was thrown off balance. Before he could regain his footing, Angel had thrust herself at the doctor, pounding wildly at his chest with her clenched fists. "You didn' sabe 'e!" she screamed. "You didn' sabe 'e, 'cause 'e was a niggra!"

Alarmed by this sudden outburst of fury, Harriet tried to pull Angel away, but the doctor motioned her away. He grasped Angel's flailing fists, holding them firmly with his strong hands until her cries subsided. "No, my dear," he said. His voice was very gentle. "It had nothing to do with Zach being black. I didn't save him, because I couldn't. Just as I'm incapable of saving all of the others, black and white, who die in this place. I'm not God. I can't perform miracles, though many's the time I wished I could."

Looking deeply into Angel's eyes, the doctor waited while she let out a spasm of deep sobs. "I can only stand by," he continued, "and hold their hands while they die. And that's what I did for your Zach. I told him about your vigil. I told him of how deeply you loved him. It was the only comfort I could give, you see. And evidently it was enough. Your Zach, he died quietly knowing that he was loved. And that's more than I can say for most of them."

Angel fell against the doctor's chest, but this time she did not pound at him with her fists. Shaken by painful sobs, she could say nothing. The physician wrapped his arms gently around her and let her cry. When her sobs subsided, he handed her over to Samuel.

"Beggin' yo' pa'don, suh," said Harriet as she motioned the doctor aside. They moved a few paces away from the sorrowing pair of mourners.

"Kin we habe de boy's body?" Harriet asked quietly.

The doctor shook his head. "I'm sorry," he said, "but it's not possible. They have to cremate the remains, you know. Even after death, a victim can transmit this disease. We fight it as hard as we can, but—well, sometimes it's a losing battle. Then all we can do is try to keep it from spreading."

Harriet glanced up toward the house, her eyes following the black column of smoke rising above the roof line. She nodded her understanding. "Es dere anyt'ing dat we kin take back fo' burial?" she asked.

The doctor lifted his eyebrows and shrugged his shoulders. But then he turned and walked back toward the gate. He motioned for the guard and whispered something to him. When he came back, he merely nodded in Harriet's direction. Then remounting the old horse, the doctor rode away.

It was some hours later before another orderly dressed in a white, but terribly stained, coat, came walking down the oyster shell drive. In his hands he carried a small wooden box filled with Zach's ashes. The gate was opened once more. The orderly walked slowly toward Angel. He held the box out to her, and when she took it, he straightened himself up and saluted her smartly.

Stunned and speechless, Angel looked at the orderly, then dropped her eyes on the box. Someone had carefully placed a shiny gold badge on the box. It was imprinted with the crossed swords insignia of the infantry, and the letters *U.S.* stood out boldly on its face. Angel looked at the badge, then let out an animal-like cry. Tears spilled unchecked down her face and dropped wetly onto the front of her shift. She turned to face Samuel and Harriet. "I wants ta take 'e home now," she said. "I wants ta take Zach back home ta Coosaw."

They buried Zach's ashes in the old slave cemetery on the banks of the Coosaw River. His grave was next to Gullah Jim's, the man who had been the closest thing to a father Zach had ever known. A contingent of men from the First Carolina Volunteers came out for the funeral. And with them was Colonel Higginson, Zach's commanding officer. No one was surprised to see the shimmer of tears in the colonel's eyes as Zach's small box of remains was laid to rest in the moist ground of Coosaw.

A bugler played taps with slow, mournful tones. There were the usual sharp salutes of rifles being fired at the sky. Then Colonel Higginson stepped toward Angel and handed her the folded American flag. The flag had been draped over the oxcart that had carried Zach's small box of ashes to the cemetery. It had seemed foolish at first to use the cart, but as this was a tradition that the Gullah people of the Sea Islands had long used, Angel felt it was fitting.

Colonel Higginson's voice was strong and controlled when he spoke to the young woman who stood tall despite her twisted feet and terrible grief. "He was a good soldier, my dear," said the colonel. "The very best there was! His country is proud of him."

Then, as always, the people who had known and loved Zach best gathered around his grave to sing him their last farewell:

> Goodbye, brudder, goodbye, brudder;
> Now God bless you, now God bless you.
> We part in de body, but we meet in de spirit,
> We'll meet in de heaben, in de blessed kingdom.
> Goodbye, brudder, goodbye, brudder;
> If I don't see you more, now God bless you.

It was a solemn company that walked back to the grounds of the Weldon Oaks Plantation. So many gone, thought Samuel. So very many gone! Old ones. Young ones. The weak. The strong. Death has no favorites.

Samuel glanced up toward the house that sat on the wide lawns. In his mind's eye, he could see the children who had lived there, both black and white. He could hear their voices and the sounds of their laughter. Then, as clear as a bell, he heard the strident voice of young Gilly Weldon calling out to his little "daily give" servant:

"Zach! Zach, where are you?" the voice called.

"I's right he'e, Massa Gilly."

"How many times have I told you not to call me Massa Gilly? Now you stop that, you hear?"

"Yes, suh, Massa Gilly. I yeddy what you say."

And then they would laugh. They would lift their fishing poles over their shoulders, and they would walk down the path to the river, laughing and chattering together just as if they had always been the very best of friends.

Chapter 10

Uncle Billy's Bummers

(November to December 1864)

Then sang we a song of our chieftain,
That echoed over river and lea;
And the stars of our banner shone brighter
When Sherman marched down to the sea!*

Gilly sat on the porch of the Russells' town house with the *Savannah Daily Morning News* spread out across his lap. He caught his breath when he read the headlines, then let out a sharp whistle.

ATLANTA FALLS TO SHERMAN
CITY LEFT IN SMOLDERING RUINS
60,000 TROOPS HEADED FOR THE SEA

"Ellen!" he called, his voice sharp and urgent. "Come out here! There's something you must see!" Hesitating, he listened for her quick step. "Have you seen the morning papers?" he shouted before she could even reach the hallway.

Ellen Russell appeared at the open door. "Can't it wait, Gilly? Mama and I have breakfast nearly ready and—" Her admonition was cut short when she saw Gilly's ashen face.

"Why, what *ever* is the matter, Gilly?" Dropping the towel she had been drying her hands with, Ellen rushed out onto the porch. "Land sakes!" she exclaimed. "You look like you've seen a ghost!"

Gilly held the paper out to her. "Here," he said, "read it for yourself."

Grasping the newspaper, Ellen looked at it quickly, then let out a gasp. "Oh no!" she cried as she dropped heavily into a nearby chair. "This can't be true! It simply can't be true!"

Gilly shook his head. "Oh, but it *is* true, Ellen, and I'm not in the least surprised. I've seen this coming for some time now."

"Bu—but surely they'll stop him, Gilly!" Ellen's face had gone bone white. "Our army certainly will stop him!"

"No, I don't think so," Gilly said evenly. "If we couldn't stop Sherman in Atlanta, we're not going to stop him anywhere else—not in Georgia, at least. And now he's heading in our direction, Ellen. Heaven help us when he gets here!"

Ellen's pretty face crumpled. "No, Gilly!" she cried. "You mustn't say that." Hesitating, she studied the front-page drawing of Atlanta gutted by flames. "He—he wouldn't do this to us, would he? He wouldn't burn Savannah?"

Gilly said nothing, but the expression on his face clearly told her what he thought.

"Oh, dear, surely they'll stop him before he gets to Savannah!"

Alarmed by the look of sheer terror on Ellen's face, Gilly jumped up and put his arms around her shoulders. He had known Ellen Russell for only a few weeks, but in that short time, he had seen ample evidence of her fortitude. She, like the rest of Savannah's citizens, had felt the pinch of the Union's blockade on the coastal city. But this new reaction—this cowering sort of fear—was startling to Gilly. He had not meant to frighten Ellen so badly. Still, she should be warned of the danger, for it was very real.

Gilly's feelings for Ellen Russell had grown from a mild attraction to something approaching adoration in the past several weeks. After their initial meeting, he and Ellen had begun to see a great deal of each other. Mary Russell, Ellen's mother, had liked Gilly from the start and had readily welcomed him into her gracious Savannah home. Indeed, it was obvious that she was encouraging a match between the two young people, a turn of events that Gilly readily welcomed. He felt comfortable and at home with the Russells. The trauma that he had experienced over the past few years seemed to fade into the background when he was with them.

With her delicate figure and pixielike features, Ellen Russell seemed more of a child than a nineteen-year-old woman. Gilly was enraptured by her. He wanted nothing more than to make Ellen his wife, but for the time being, propriety and the war seemed to dictate otherwise. And now here he was, frightening her half to death with this news of General Sherman. He should know better than to tamper with Ellen's fluctuating emotions, especially at a time like this. Hardly a week had passed since she'd learned of her older brother's death in Tennessee. Devastated by the news, she had been crying for days. And now this!

How rapidly things were changing, thought Gilly. They had been so happy—almost carefree—when they'd first met. Despite the deprivations in the city, a social life of sorts was still possible. He and Ellen had been introduced to each other at a fund-raising fete sponsored by the Ladies Guild of Savannah, one of many such events that galvanized the entire city into a united front. And while there had been nothing pretentious about the party, it had brought out a prestigious group of Savannah's citizens.

As a newly appointed ensign in the popular Savannah Squadron, Gilly had found himself a welcome guest. In fact, once the word got around that he had fought in the Battle of Port Royal Sound, had been wounded and captured, and had then made a daring escape from the Hilton Head prison stockade, Gilly's popularity soared. He had became a hero, eagerly sought after by the women of Savannah, especially those with marriageable-age daughters. But once Gilly set his eyes on Ellen Russell, all other young women paled to insignificance.

The fund-raising events had gone unabated. With the rapid changes in naval warfare brought on by the introduction of ironclad ships, the Confederacy was in dire need of a new navy.

Savannah stood in the very forefront of this rapid push for ship-building. And with Federal forces massing on her very door-step, via the sea, the city eagerly welcomed the young naval officers like Gilly who came to man the newly built ships.

Ellen's mother, Mary, was a tireless worker for the cause. Having lost her husband early in the war, and now more recently her son, she had learned to veil her sorrow with the cloak of hard work. Thus, if the presence of her petite daughter at the many fetes and balls enticed young naval officers to participate in her fund-raising efforts, then all the better.

But now the war news was rapidly turning bad, and all the efforts to defend Savannah from the sea suddenly seemed wasted. Gilly shuddered at the thought of what was coming. It was one thing for the city's womenfolk to hold patriotic social events but quite another for them to be caught in the middle of a military siege. And since he was now officially courting Ellen, Gilly felt that he had every right to take a proprietary interest in her welfare.

Standing on the porch with his arms around Ellen's quaking shoulders, he decided that something must be done immediately to get her out of the city. Turning her slowly around, he grasped her arms and forced her to look into his eyes. "Ellen, I didn't mean to frighten you," he said, trying to keep his voice slow and steady, "but you must understand the nature of Sherman's warfare. Quite honestly, I feel that you and your mother should leave this city as soon as possible."

"Oh no, Gilly!" Ellen looked at him with a renewed expression of shock in her eyes. "It can't be that bad! I'm sure we'll be quite safe here. Why, Mama says that—"

"I don't care what your mother says, Ellen." Now Gilly was truly alarmed by Ellen's apparent denial of the seriousness of this situation. He must make her understand! Picking up the paper, he pointed to one of the lead stories:

Uncle Billy, as his men call him, is even now leading a vast army of his bummers across Georgia. They are

men without principles, having regard for neither soldiers nor civilians, men nor women, old nor young. They
burn, loot, and plunder at will, much of the time under
their general's direct orders. Sherman has vowed that
he will bring the South to her knees, and nothing, not
even mass slaughter or total devastation, will desist
him from this dastardly pursuit.

Ellen looked at Gilly in horror. Fear etched white circles
around her eyes and pulled at the corners of her mouth. "Wha—
what shall we do?" she asked in dismay.

"You must do just as I've said," Gilly insisted. "You and your
mother must pack your things and leave this city as quickly as
possible."

"Where, Gilly? Where would we go?" Ellen was almost beside herself with worry, but this was a question that Gilly had
not yet thought out. "Perhaps to Charleston," he said hesitantly.
"The trains are still running quite regularly. But you mustn't
wait too long. Once Sherman gets to the railroad lines, he'll
make quick work of them."

"But I'll never convince Mama to leave!" wailed Ellen. "She's
adamant about staying here in the city no matter what happens."

Gilly patted Ellen's shoulder. "You'll convince her, Ellen. I'm
sure she'll leave when she hears about Sherman and his bummers."

"I think not, Mr. Weldon! I'm not in the habit of giving in to
bullies!"

Gilly spun around. He had not heard Mary Russell open the
door and come out onto the porch. Though small in stature like
her daughter, Mary had a commanding presence that left little
room for doubt as to who was in charge. And now her face was
so filled with stubborn determination that Gilly actually found
himself stepping backward.

Mary Russell reached out and picked up the paper. With
her eyes moving rapidly back and forth across the page, she
scanned the columns. Then, still without comment, she leafed

through the rest of the paper. That she was startled by the approach of Sherman's army was quite evident from the tight line of her lips. But Mary Russell was made of stern stuff. She had endured too much sorrow, suffered too many losses, to give up her home without a fight. And to embark upon the life of a refugee, to be shuffled from place to place by the ever-widening effects of the war, was completely beyond her ken.

No, Savannah was Mary Russell's home and had been for all of her life. Three generations of Russells had dwelt in this same house on Abercorn Street. Their string of cotton warehouses along the waterfront had given them a very comfortable income, and their business interests in the growing city had earned them an enviable reputation. Mary was not about to end the family's succession over the approach of an army of a mere sixty thousand men, bummers or no.

Swallowing hard as he built up his nerve, Gilly decided that for just this once, Mary Russell must listen to reason. He took a step or two in her direction, then pointed to a column on the bottom right side of the paper's front page. "You'd best read what it says here, Mrs. Russell. As I've told Ellen, Sherman is a commander with little compassion for civilians, and his army consists of the most hard-bitten Yankees ever to have come out of the North. Look what it says here." Gilly pointed to the article's screaming headline: **SHERMAN COMMITTED TO TOTAL WARFARE!** "You *do* know what that means, don't you, Mrs. Russell?" Gilly was no longer concerned about frightening Ellen. It was Mary Russell who must be confronted now. If she cared nothing for her own safety, then surely she must be made to see the need for protecting that of her daughter.

"Mrs. Russell." Gilly's voice was level but stern. "This means that General Sherman intends to make war upon the entire civilian population of Georgia. It means that he'll give his troops free rein to do whatever they wish. They'll burn their way across this state, and when they get to Savannah, it will all break loose here as well!"

"Yes," said Mary Russell very quietly, "I imagine that's possible. But I also think that there are ways to avert catastrophe."

"Ways to avert it?" Gilly was beside himself with frustration. Why couldn't he make this stubborn woman see what was coming upon them? With shaking hands, he grasped at the paper again and thumped his forefinger on the story that told of Atlanta's ordeals.

"Look! I beg of you to look!" he shouted. "Not even the dead were left in peace. Sherman's rabble went so far as to dig up the very graves in Atlanta's cemeteries. They pulled corpses from their coffins—stripped them bare of the valuables they'd been buried with. He's a monster, I tell you! This Sherman is an absolute monster!"

Mary Russell's face was white and drawn, but still she remained unyielding. "Perhaps these are just inflammatory stories, Gilly. The press has a way of doing that sort of thing. And I personally know folks who were acquainted with Mr. Sherman when he lived here in the South. He did, you know. He has many friends and acquaintances in this city. Perhaps he's not really the monster the papers make him out to be."

Gilly threw up his hands in disgust.

Reaching out to him, Mary Russell tried to calm Gilly's frayed nerves. "I have no intention of running away from Sherman," she said emphatically. "And I have every confidence that our city's leaders can negotiate some kind of peace with this man."

Exasperated by Mary's stubbornness, Gilly tried to compromise with her. "All right! All right! Stay if you must, Mrs. Russell, but at least send Ellen away. She's just a girl! Who knows what they'll do to her!"

Mary's face once again filled with anger. "Gilly, do you really think you need to convince me of how dangerous this situation is? I'm not a fool, you know. Nor am I another 'Lot's wife.' But, my dear boy, precisely where would you have me send Ellen?"

Gilly rubbed the flat of his hand down the back of his head. "To Charleston, possibly, or to—"

"Ah yes, I see." Mary Russell shook her head in dismay. "Dear boy, would you have me send Ellen right into the clutches of these invaders? And do you know how many raids have been made on the Charleston-Savannah line as of late?"

She spun around and walked to the porch railing, then turned to face him once more. "Or perhaps you would have me send her by ship—run the blockade and get killed in the process!" Her voice was filled with sarcasm now. "Has it entered your mind, Gilly, that after Sherman has his way with Savannah, he might just as well head right on to Charleston and do the very same thing there? And where would we run to then, Gilly? How long would you have us put off the inevitable tide of defeat?"

Gilly slumped into a nearby chair. She was right, of course. Mary Russell was right. The people of Savannah were prisoners in their own city, locked in as tightly as though they were behind bars. If the war became unbearable, he had thought about taking himself further south into the wilds of Florida, but it was unthinkable that he should drag Ellen along on such a perilous journey. And with Sherman's army coming straight at them from the west—well, that direction, too, was out of the question. Shaking his head wearily, Gilly looked up at Mary Russell with pleading eyes. "What can we do?" he asked. "Whatever can we do?"

Poor Gilly! thought Mary. *This war has brought him nothing but one tragedy after another.* After finally making it to Savannah and thinking that he'd found a place of refuge, now once again his world was falling apart at his feet. He had managed to outsmart death at least twice in his young life. How much longer would his luck hold?

Mary Russell knew of Gilly's feelings, and her heart ached for him as though he were her own son. She longed to give him some word of encouragement—some inner strength to hold onto in all the fearful times yet to come.

Sitting down next to the young naval officer, Mary reached out and placed her hands over his clenched fists. "You've done your best, Gilly," she said, "and we love you for that. But the truth is, we've really got no choices now. We must stay here."

Her voice grew very quiet. "You mustn't worry about us, though. You see, Ellen and I have learned to put our trust in God. He's carried us through so much already, and He'll carry us through this too."

Gilly nodded but said nothing. He felt that somehow he had failed Ellen. What must she think of him now, carrying on this way? Well, he'd just have to prove to her that he was made of as stern of stuff as her mother was. And when the time came, when Sherman and his vile hoard overran the city, Gilly would make certain that he was here to protect Ellen. If he had to desert to do it, he would!

Over the next few weeks, the news of General Sherman's sweep across the red earth of Georgia was followed by the citizens of Savannah with a growing sense of horror. The destruction left in the wake of his army was even more appalling than anyone had imagined. And to make matters worse, it was soon obvious that the Confederate forces attempting to stop the onslaught were little more than a nuisance factor. It took less than a month for the advancing army to reach the western outskirts of Savannah. And by that time, everyone in the city knew that Savannah was lost.

There followed an event that left Gilly even more shaken and guilt-ridden than any of his previous misadventures. For the defenders of Savannah, there were only two choices. Either they must surrender themselves to General Sherman, or they must slink away through the marshy waterways and leave the civilians of the city, mostly women and children, completely at the mercy of the enemy. And in the end, it was the latter choice that was made. It was a ghastly thing to do, but if the Confederate forces of the area wished to survive in order to continue their fight, it was the only choice possible.

Gilly was aboard a small tender ship known as the *Resolute,* when on the night of December 20, 1864, he and his fellow shipmates watched Savannah's defenders march across the hastily built pontoon bridges to the South Carolina shore. They had strewn the bridges with rice straw to muffle the sound of their passage. Their women and children, their old and their invalid, were left behind.

Gilly had last seen Ellen that very morning, but now her face seemed little more than a blur in his memory. No, he hadn't intended things to happen this way, but somewhere along the line he had lost his nerve. His memories of the Hilton Head prison stockade had resurfaced and struck him with a vengeance. The smells of it, the sounds of it, the terror of dying in such a place, had all become too real again.

Haunted by Ellen's fear and grief, Gilly had come as close as he ever would to actually deserting. Oh yes, he had thought about signing the Union's loyalty oath back then when he'd been a prisoner of war, but that was completely different. Then, he had had only himself to think of. But now he had Ellen to worry over, and how did he just turn his back and leave her to face the monstrous things that might happen when Sherman's troops descended upon the city?

The one thing that was carrying him through all of this shame and agony was Mary Russell's insistence that God Himself was on her side. That and the fact that he could never look either himself or Ellen in the eye again if he had deserted. Seeing the courage of this indomitable woman, Gilly had felt terribly humbled. She had been a wall of strength for him during those final days. And though it was terribly painful to think of, Gilly couldn't help but compare Mary's tenacity under pressure with the weakness he had seen in his own mother. Through some mysterious process, Mary had managed to give her daughter this same courage. It was a revelation to Gilly, for if and when the day came when he and Ellen did marry, then surely he could ask for no better dowry.

On the morning of December 21, 1864, Sherman and his troops marched into Savannah. Hardly a shot was fired in the city, for just as Mary Russell had predicted, Savannah's leading citizens managed to negotiate a peaceful settlement with "Uncle" Billy Sherman. And after all of the damage wreaked by his invading army as they cut their way across Georgia,

Savannah at least won a victory of sorts by simply capitulating. Unfortunately, it was to be one of the last such gentle acts on the terrible road to the South's final defeat.

---

* The chorus of "Sherman's March to the Sea" was a song composed by Adjutant S. H. M. Byers while he was a prisoner of war at Camp Sorghum in Columbia, South Carolina. Byers handed the words of his song to Sherman when the general entered the city of Columbia on the morning of February 17, 1865 (taken from *Memoirs of General W. T. Sherman* [New York: D. Appleton & Co., 1875], 2:282).

Chapter 11

Do Remember Me

(January–February 1865)

The sound of drums rumbled across the waters surrounding Beaufort as the first of the ships carrying General Sherman's troops moved slowly upriver. Seasick and anxious to reach solid ground, Uncle Billy's bummers pressed themselves against the railings and eyed the waiting crowd. The rolling mist lifted just as the ship approached its mooring, and the town itself was revealed. The weary campaigners, mouths agape, took one look and forgot the agony of their latest ordeal. Beaufort was the very epitome of what they had been hoping for ever since Savannah. Not even the obvious presence of Federal troops could dampen their hopes that now, at last, they might once more experience the sheer joy of unrestricted plundering!

Indeed, Beaufort had a prosperous and well-heeled look. Business seemed to be booming on the main thoroughfare. Piles of provisions for the encamped army were stacked high along the waterfront. Crates and bundles of confiscated goods, those that had not as yet been shipped North, were even now being loaded onto waiting cargo ships. The occupying army and its hangers-on were living well. While the coastal blockade was effectively strangling the rest of the South, this tiny bit of Union-held land was suffering very few privations. Sherman's bummers saw little reason to concern themselves with the right or wrong of this imbalance, as long as they got their share of the rich booty.

Beaufort, despite being twice ravaged, once by its freed slaves and then by the occupying Union forces, had, with a good deal of outside help, managed to recoup at least a shade of its original elegance. Its genteel homes and flourishing business establishments now belonged to Northerners, but the languid Southern climate still worked its same subtle magic on the town. The battlefields of the war were far distant. There was the military presence for protection. The use of the large and once-opulent homes for hospitals and surgeries assured their ultimate preservation. The sum total of all this was that Beaufort's new citizenry had developed a pleasant though somewhat precarious sense of well-being.

And now, with the approach of these conquerors of Georgia, there was even a growing enthusiasm for the war effort. A reputation for wanton thievery had proceeded Sherman's bummers, but here in Beaufort, they could hardly be classified as the enemy! Even the suspicions that the fiery rampage through Georgia had so hardened them that they no longer viewed pillage as a crime seemed inappropriate under the present circumstances. Sadly, this trusting attitude was about to leave Beaufort wide open for another wholesale plundering. But for the present, at least, that worry had been set aside. With the coming of Sherman's army, the long, hard years of war seemed to be at last winding down.

Mindful of the damage to his reputation that his troops might cause, General Sherman had taken some diversionary actions. He wanted no trouble while his men were in Beaufort, but even he recognized that they were getting hard to control. That he had managed to keep them in line during their stay in Savannah had been nothing short of miraculous. If Savannah *had* fallen to the torch, few Northerners would have complained. But here, in a town already flying the Union flag, it was imperative that nothing go amiss.

Thus, when the general discovered that Beaufort was being guarded by black troops, he gave a sigh of relief. If his men did step over the line, it could hardly be construed as a deficiency on his part. Whoever heard of a white man giving way to the orders of a black provost guard? And considering how subservient most of Georgia's Negroes had been, Sherman could hardly imagine that putting one in a Union uniform would make him in any way more forceful.

There was another factor in Sherman's favor, though its positive effects upon Beaufort were completely incidental. The greatest number of the general's troops had left Savannah and marched inland, first following the Savannah River along its marshy course, then traveling north through the sandy hills that marked the western edges of the Low Country.

It was Sherman's intention to keep the Confederate defenders of South Carolina guessing as to his ultimate objectives, and to do this, he had divided his army. The western, or left wing, after skirting along the low ridges, had made a feint toward Augusta. The troops of the right wing, the ones who were now being shipped up the coast to Beaufort, would give the appearance of readying themselves for an attack on Charleston.

It was a stunning plan, and so far it had kept even the Union forces already in Beaufort guessing. Both Augusta and Charleston would be worthy prizes of war, but Sherman had no intention of wasting his efforts on cities that no longer held any strategic importance. He meant to go straight for South Carolina's jugular vein. It was Columbia that he wanted—the birthplace of the secessionist movement. And if on the way, he left another great swath of destruction, all the better. He felt that the South had asked for this war; thus he would give it to her in good measure. Few of the military hierarchy waiting on the docks on this misty morning while Sherman's seagoing troops began to disembark had any idea of the general's bold intention. It had been a well-kept secret only because William T. Sherman seldom consulted even his own staff officers about his military strategies.

But there had been one small slip-up. Someone had overheard a hurried conversation and had judged aright what Sherman was about to do. Luckily, that person was neither a spy nor a traitor. He was a young man of honor, and he had only one pressing concern about the general's plans for Columbia. Medical Corpsman Jonathan Franklin had a debt to pay to a young woman now living in Columbia. More than once she had saved his life, and now he must return that favor, for if Columbia was going to go the way of Atlanta, then surely she was in the gravest of danger!

Perhaps it was only luck that had put Jonathan on duty in the hospital that night when one of Sherman's most trusted officers had been brought in with a bad case of dysentery. Then again, perhaps it was providence. At any rate, the officer had been put to bed in a private room well away from the hectic activity going on in the rest of the hospital. Along about midnight, Jonathan had gone in to check on the man. Finding that the officer was sleeping only fitfully, he settled down on a pallet of laundry stacked behind a wide screen with the intention of being close by if the sick man should need his help.

The past evening had been especially wearing. Jonathan was near exhaustion. Without intending to, he had drifted off to sleep. It was the overpowering odor of General Sherman's ever-present cigar that finally awakened him. And as the two officers were already well into a whispered and obviously top-secret conversation, it seemed rather foolhardy to make his presence known. He'd most likely be accused of spying. So lying perfectly still, hardly daring to breathe, Jonathan became privy to General Sherman's plans for Columbia.

And now, just two days later, he stood beside Angel on Beaufort's waterfront and watched as one after the other of the transport ships unloaded their human cargo. Like everyone else in Beaufort, Angel had wanted to witness this great arrival, but Jonathan had been concerned about her safety in the jostling crowd. Samuel was away on some secret business, so it was left to him to see that Angel was properly protected.

Then again, Jonathan had another reason for wanting to spend this time with Angel. After much careful thought, he had hatched up a plan for saving Laura May. But if it was to work properly, he would need Angel's help. With her close contacts among the missionaries on the Sea Islands, Angel was in a good position to set the proper wheels in motion.

Unfortunately, since Zach's untimely death, Angel had become completely unpredictable. Jonathan had no idea how she would take to his plans, so he needed to broach the subject with care. For several minutes now, he had been skirting around the issue. Frustratingly, Angel ignored everything he said. In fact, Jonathan was beginning to doubt that she was even aware of his presence.

Exasperated by this lack of attentiveness, Jonathan finally decided to just blurt it all out. "Listen, Angel," he said, his voice trying to rise above the shouts of the cheering crowd, "when General Sherman resumes his march, I'm going with him!"

Angel dropped her raised hand and turned to stare into Jonathan's face. "Hab you done lost yo' mind, Jonat'an! You es still as weak as a sick cat. What fo' you wanna go traipsin' 'round de country wid de likes ob dat riff-raff? Hain't you had 'nuff troubles as et es?"

Jonathan shrugged his shoulders and laughed. "Angel, I'm as fit as ever. And Sherman's men aren't really a bad sort. A bit exuberant, perhaps, but—"

"Dey es de debil's own, an' you knows dat, Jonat'an!"

"Listen, Angel." Jonathan's voice turned plaintive, "Just hear me out on this. What I have in mind is as important to you as it is to me."

"Well, what es et den?" Angel asked, her tone severe with irritation. "What be so impo'tant dat you es willin' ta risk loosin' yo' life ober?"

"Oh, come now, Angel!" Jonathan was growing increasingly impatient. "Joining up with Sherman's army wouldn't be *that* dangerous. Look at those fellows out there. They're as robust and well-fed as a bunch of new recruits. Why, he's brought them all the way through Georgia and hardly lost a man! And what if there is a little danger? I'm still in the army, aren't I? I have no right to hide myself away here when other men are in the thick of the fighting. Besides, what I have in mind would be well worth the risk."

Angel stood silently waiting for his explanation, but Jonathan suddenly seemed hesitant. He rubbed his chin, then looked furtively around to make sure no one was listening. Then he pulled her off to one side. "Angel," he said in a low whisper, "this isn't common knowledge, so I'd be obliged if you wouldn't mention it to anyone. But, well, there's a rumor going around that Sherman intends to head straight for Columbia when he leaves Beaufort. Most people think that he's going up the coast to invade Charleston, and for the time being, it's best they keep believing that. Do you understand what I mean?"

"How does you know dis, Jonat'an?"

"I—well—I just happened to overhear a conversation. I didn't mean to, you understand, but it's a good thing that I did."

Perplexed, Angel found herself speechless. What was Jonathan getting at? Why should such rumors be important to them? Hadn't they had troubles enough? Now here he was, thinking up some harebrained scheme that was sure to get him killed.

"You don't understand, do you, Angel?" Jonathan was getting more annoyed. "You see, Sherman is just itching to punish this state, and the city of Columbia in particular. After all, wasn't it those fire-eating politicians up there who started this whole miserable war in the first place?"

Angel narrowed her eyes. "An' dey es de ones what held you pris'ner, hain't dat so, Jonat'an? All dis time, you bin-a jes holdin' hatred inside ob you like a rolled-up snake. An' now dat you got de chance, you wants ta go back up dere an' ease dat hatred some by killin' off a few ob dem Seceshes, huh." There was scorn in her voice. Somehow she had expected more of Jonathan than this.

"No!" he insisted. "No, you've got it all wrong. I have no desire for personal vengeance. What happened to me is over and done with. Revenge wouldn't change anything."

Passing a hand across his eyes, Jonathan shook his head. "But I will tell you this, Angel. It would be a real pleasure to have a hand in liberating Camp Sorghum." He sighed deeply, then shook his head again. "But, no, I have other and far more pressing reasons to return to Columbia."

Still mystified, Angel waited for further explanations. She couldn't imagine why Jonathan was taking so long to come out with his plans.

"Don't you see?" he said, his voice quiet but firm. "It's for Laura May's sake. I want to find her, Angel. I want to find her and get her out of there before it's too late. You know what happened in Atlanta. Can you just imagine what Sherman's troops will do to Columbia when they get there? Laura May—and everybody else in the city, for that matter—is in the gravest danger! This won't be another Savannah. Blood will flow, Angel, a lot of it! And Sherman's men are just itching to see another city burned to the ground!"

A look of fear crossed Angel's face. "Jonat'an, does you really beliebe dat? Es Massa Sherman gwanna let dat happen ta Columbia?"

Jonathan only looked sadly into her eyes. "He might take pity on the place, Angel, but I don't think for a minute that that will stop the inevitable from happening. Sherman may want to control his troops, but I doubt he'll be able to. All they have to do is march past Camp Sorghum. They'll take one look at those holes in the ground and the skeletal men who were forced to live in them, and they'll want revenge in the worst kind of way. And who would blame them? It's a disaster in the making, Angel, and Laura May will be caught right in the middle of it!"

Angel pressed her hands against her face. "Oh, me, oh, my," she moaned. "Dat po' chil'! Hain't she neber gwanna hab an end ob troubles?" Eyes streaming with tears, Angel looked forlornly up at Jonathan. "Me an' Maum Beezie, we ben-a prayin' fo' dat gal till weuns hab most run outta wu'ds. But somehow, et don' seem ta do no good. I ben-a t'inkin', Jonat'an, dat Gawd, 'E don' list'n ta me no mo'. Fust 'E took Laura May away, den Zach. I musta done sumpin' terrible bad fo' Gawd ta punish me so!"

"Oh, Angel!" Jonathan reached out and touched Angel's shoulders. "You mustn't blame either yourself or God for any of this. What has happened is the result of evil, pure and simple. But it wasn't your evil—and it certainly wasn't God's! This war has been a long time in the making. Human slavery is what caused it—greedy men wanting to own others for personal gain. And now it's time to pay up—the slave owners for what they've done, and the Northerners for what they didn't do."

Jonathan let out a deep sigh. "Folks like you and Laura May," he said, "why, you're the victims. It has to be set straight, Angel, and I guess that's another reason why I want to go along with Sherman. I've been sitting around here thinking only of myself for far too long, and now it's time I corrected that."

Angel sniffled and wiped her face with the back of her sleeve. "Den you t'ink dat Gawd still hears mah prayers, Jonat'an?"

Despite his frustrations with this conversation, Jonathan had to smile. "Of course, He does, Angel! What's more, I have a feeling that He's about to answer them. You see, maybe this is what He's had in mind all along. I mean, me going back to Columbia to find Laura May. It's an interesting thought, isn't it?"

Turning slowly, Angel and Jonathan made their way back toward the hospital house. Angel would be on duty soon. The arrival of the new troops made no change in the needs of the sick and wounded.

"You t'ink dis'll work, Jonat'an?" Angel asked as they walked along. "How es you gwanna be able ta find Laura May befo' sumpin' terrible happens ta she?"

Jonathan looked away, for this was a thought that had been bothering him too. There was always the possibility of failure. Columbia was a big city filled to bursting with refugees. And even without the mass confusion that an invasion would surely cause, he hadn't the first clue as to where he should start looking for Laura May. That she lived with her mother and a cousin somewhere in the center of the city he was certain. But he had never been to the house.

Jonathan's memories of Columbia were, at best, very sketchy. His images of the place were a jumble, all mixed up with the scenes of his entry into the city as a prisoner of war. A mob of angry people pushing and shoving, shouting insults, a host of little boys, both black and white, prodding him with sticks, throwing stones. And then suddenly, there was Laura May, a girl in her teens caught in the press. Frightened eyes. A face gone white with terror. He had reached out to grasp her arm when she was pushed against him. And from that point on, fate seemed to have intervened.

Jonathan had not forgotten that face. Through all of the terrible months in the prison stockade, it was Laura May's gentle face and frightened eyes that had given him courage. Not everyone in the South was filled with rage. Not everyone was bent upon destroying him.

And then, wonder of all wonders, like an angel of mercy, she had come to the prison. Bringing food. Bringing hope. And several weeks later, bringing a chance to escape. How could he forget that? It was a debt that he must repay, but not out of pure duty. Laura May's face had done something to him. Perhaps it was love at first sight.

But where would he find her? And how? He dare not share such worries with Angel, for she was already filled with doubts. And he certainly didn't have the heart to tell her how hopeless his whole plan seemed when he stepped back and really looked at it.

To Jonathan's surprise, Angel had somehow followed the circuitous route of his thoughts. They had reached the hospital. Before going in, she stopped on the walkway to look up at him. The questions were there on her face, but then, before even asking them, she came up with the answers. "Effen you es really goin' ta Columbia," she said, "den you es gwanna hafta take somebody wid you what kin show you de way. An' as et jes' so happens, I know de bery pusson."

"No, Angel." Jonathan had no idea why he suddenly felt so stubborn. A matter of pride, perhaps. "This is something I've got to do on my own. It's going to be dangerous enough for me. I can't jeopardize somebody else's life."

But Angel had a stubborn streak of her own. "Now you listen he'e ta me, Jonat'an. Dis hain't no time fo' ta get all puffed up like a peacock! What effen et happens dat you kyan't find Laura May befo' dis rabble gets ta tearin' dat city apa't? An' mayhap you won' eben hab de time ta look, enty? Den what es you gwanna do?"

"I-I don't know," answered Jonathan. "I hadn't really thought about it." He felt chagrined, knowing perfectly well that she had read him rightly.

"Seems ta me dat you hain't really taught 'bout nuttin' bery careful," said Angel, her voice filled with reproach. Angel could be very hard on a person who acted the least bit scatterbrained. "What I es sayin' es dat I gots de pusson what knows puzactly where Laura May es. Dis he'e es an' ol' colo'd man what's been bringin' messages back an' fort' atween weuns. You takes um wid you, Jonat'an, an' you hain't gwanna waste no time pokin' 'round where et won' do no good."

Jonathan nodded. Angel was right, of course. Time would be at a premium. And it certainly would make things easier if he could go straight to where Laura May was living.

"All right, Angel, let me think this out for a bit. But you'll have plenty of time to plot out my whole trip for me. The rest of Sherman's army is sloshing around somewhere south of here, so there'll be no rushing off to Columbia for a while yet. Besides, I don't even know if the good general will have me. I'll probably have to find someone who knows how to pull a few strings."

Angel nodded, but her thoughts were already racing far ahead of Jonathan's words. She knew that he could never keep up with an army if he were on foot. And Sherman's soldiers were trail-hardened campaigners, well seasoned by the rigors of marching long distances through the worst of conditions. Though Jonathan was much improved, he was still weak from his long prison ordeal. Why, wondered Angel, should the general even want to take Jonathan along? Outside of the fact that he had already covered the distance between Columbia and Beaufort in making good his escape, he had little else to recommend him.

Several days passed before they saw each other again. Angel was extremely busy in the hospital. More and more wounded men were coming in now. It was heartbreaking to see them, to know that so little could be done to relieve their pain and suffering. And finding qualified physicians and surgeons for the black hospital was always a problem. Prejudice ran rampant in the army's medical unit.

But Angel did take the time to make some inquiries. She learned that the field ambulance service was always in need of attendants, especially drivers. Was Sherman planning on taking some ambulances along on the line of march? Surely he'd have to. The further her inquiries went on this line, the more she realized that this was the answer to at least one of their problems.

A week passed before she got to talk to Jonathan again. He was as discouraged as she had ever seen him. No, he had not been able to make any headway with the officers he had talked to. No, he hadn't even spoken to Sherman yet; the general was somewhere to the southwest of Beaufort.

Finally, Angel broke the good news. It was all arranged. Jonathan would drive an ambulance wagon at the back of the line of march. He'd have to get some quick training in handling mules, and he'd have to know at least the basics of emergency medical care in the field, but that would be easy enough to accomplish. He was already a medical corpsman in one of the hospital houses. And as for getting the proper clearance from General Sherman, well, Angel had even gotten that into the works. Amazed by her efficiency and persistence, Jonathan could only shake his head in wonder.

"I don't know why I didn't just turn this whole thing over to you in the first place," he said. "Then perhaps I would have gotten a good night's sleep."

It was late January before Sherman's army commenced its march, this time heading to the northwest. Fearful of what was to come, South Carolina's defenders tried desperately to marshal their forces, but the generals in charge of the Confederate army could offer no real assistance. Robert E. Lee needed every man he could get to hold Virginia. Braxton Bragg had already siphoned off a large chunk of the available manpower for the fighting in North Carolina. The state of Georgia was in a shambles, its surviving volunteers rendered useless by the decree of some shortsighted politicians who insisted that their militia must not cross the state line. Thus, Columbia was left virtually defenseless and completely at the mercy of the approaching army.

Riding far behind the line of march in an ambulance wagon that had never been designed to negotiate swamplands, Jonathan began to despair that he would ever see Columbia. There were numerous skirmishes along the way, all of which called for his services. Time and again he was ordered to take the wounded back to Beaufort, but so far he had managed to weasel his way back into the line of march. He thought about the horrors of Camp Sorghum and the friends he had left behind there. He worried over Laura May, tortured by thoughts of what might happen to her if he did not get to Columbia in time.

Mile upon mile, through mosquito-infested swamps and moisture-laden woodlands, the army moved forward, never doubting that the city of Columbia would be theirs for the taking. Plantation homes and humble farmsteads were plundered with equal relish. Whiskey flowed freely, for this army seemed to travel better on the bottle than on its feet. Railroad lines were destroyed with the same efficiency that had been so well practiced in Georgia, with the ties burned, and the rails bent into what the men jokingly referred to as "Lincoln gimlets."

Worst of all for Jonathan was the pillage along the way. A group of bummers would enter a house where a woman and her children, alone and undefended, would plead for their meager food supply and cherished belongings to be left untouched. As often as not, the answer came in the form of profanity and curses. Violent acts were common and seldom punished. Much of the destruction was completely unnecessary: a grand piano chopped to bits while, under force, the woman of the house played upon it; a child's pet slaughtered for a bummer's amusement; the very last morsels of food taken from an already-destitute family.

At first, Jonathan thought to keep a detailed diary of the barbarous behavior of Sherman's bummers, but soon even this became offensive to him. He began to believe that if he recorded the vile acts and still continued to travel with the army, he would be as guilty as the perpetrators. A new plan began to formulate itself in his mind, or rather, an extension of his original plans. Jonathan knew that some might think of what he had in mind as desertion, but he didn't see it that way.

The fact was, Jonathan began to realize that his original ideas had been incomplete. What was he to do with Laura May once he found her—given that he *did* find her? Certainly she could not travel on with *this* army. Nor could she be left alone to once again wander the countryside as a refugee. Should he try to take her back to Beaufort? Would she even want to go with him? Having no good answers to these questions, Jonathan's mind was in a constant turmoil.

By February 10, the Union Army reached the south fork of the Edisto River, the last deep-water crossing before the approach to the capital city. For General Sherman, the impossible had been realized. Within five days, his entire force was encamped on the east bank of the Congaree River, and the battle for Columbia was about to begin.

Because he was driving the cumbersome and slow-moving ambulance wagon, Jonathan found that he was too late to witness the actual liberation of Camp Sorghum. This was a major disappointment to him, but now he was faced with another dilemma. The released prisoners of war were in dire need of medical attention. How could he possibly turn away from them for the sake of saving just one young woman. The answer was obvious: he couldn't. And so, as the ominous sounds of cannon fire echoed and reechoed across the wooded sand hills to the east of Columbia, Jonathan steeled himself to the task of serving as good Samaritan to the men with whom he had once been imprisoned. And all the time, in his mind's eye, he saw the frightened face and pleading eyes of Laura May Weldon, who was somewhere out there in that city under siege.

Chapter 12

Come Judgment Day

(February 1865)

Maude rolled up her best woolen shawl and pressed it into the already tightly packed valise. Pinching the top closed, she buckled the worn leather straps, then turned to face her cousin, Marian. "It's time to leave," she said, her expression sober. "There's not a thing in this house worth dying for." Maude never had been one to mince words.

Marian Weldon hung her head and clutched at the lace hanky lying in her lap. "But, Maude," she said, her voice a mere whisper, "it's—it's so premature." She looked up with pleading eyes. "Couldn't—couldn't we just wait and see what happens?"

"See what happens?" asked Maude.

"Yes," answered Marian. "Let's just see what happens. After all, Mister Sherman behaved like a gentleman in Savannah."

"It's *General* Sherman, Marian, and when he's in front of an army, there's very little that's gentlemanly about him. I do declare, Cousin, haven't you read the papers?"

Marian gave a deep sigh. "B-but, Maude, how do we know if those terrible things they said about him were true? Perhaps all of that talk about—about wanton brutality—perhaps it was an exaggeration to—to frighten us."

Maude simply shook her head. "Marian," she said in exasperation, "you're the closest thing to an ostrich I've ever met! Haven't we seen the refugees with our own eyes? Haven't we

131

seen the haunted, desperate looks on their faces? Their stories are true, Marian, and you know it. Why must we keep pretending? What good will it do us?"

Marian dropped her eyes to her lap. "Don't make fun of me, Maude. I'm only trying to be practical—to keep a level head."

"If you want to be practical, Marian," answered the older woman, "then go upstairs and pack your valise."

"B-but, Maude," Marian stuttered, "it really does seem just a bit premature!"

Maude had had more than enough of this foolishness. "*NO!*" she said, her voice rising with anger. "It is *not* premature, Marian. If anything, it's too late! But I'll not stand here and argue with you. If you choose to stay in this city, then so be it. *I* am leaving!"

Placing her valise on the table, Maude went to the coat rack in the front hallway. She raised herself up on tiptoe and reached for her best Sunday hat. After placing it firmly on her head, she gave it a pat, then fastened it down with a long hat pin. "Marian," she said as she returned to the table to pick up her valise, "I sincerely wish you would reconsider this, for Laura May's sake, if not for your own. I fear that you are making a very grave error in staying here."

"I—I can't do it, Maude!" Marian was on the verge of tears now. "I just can't do it!"

Touched by her cousin's distress, Maude reached out and put her hand on Marian's sagging shoulder. "Oh, my dear, I know how hard it is for you. You and Laura May have been through so much horror during this war. But you must be reasonable, now more than ever."

Marian began wringing her hanky. "But I can't, Maude. I just can't. If you'd only wait a while—a day or two—just so I can think about it."

"*NO, MARIAN!*" Maude was completely out of patience now. She slammed the table with the flat of her hand and fairly spit out the words. "I'll not wait another day. Surely you didn't think that was thunder we heard last night. It was *cannon* fire, Marian! Cannon fire! Your gentlemanly Mister Sherman means to destroy this city and everyone in it! If you wish to sit here and wait for him, then you are more than welcome to do so. But don't ask me to stay with you. I'd rather spend the rest of my days wandering the roadways than—"

Marian's eyes were taking on a wild look. Jumping up, she grasped at her cousin's hands. "You *don't* know what you're talking about, Maude! You have no idea what it's like. No roof over your head. Begging for food. Always afraid of being robbed or— or worse!"

Throughout this frantic exchange, Laura May had been sitting quietly beside her mother. Torn by what might be the best course of action, she had tried to see things through her mother's eyes. Cousin Maude was right, of course, but Mama's mind was so fragile, especially now.

Reaching out for her mother's arm, Laura May pulled her gently back down into the chair. "Please, Mama, don't get yourself all upset. Let Cousin Maude go if she wishes. You and I will stay here, just like you said. We'll think things over and decide what's best when you're feeling stronger."

It was the wrong thing to say, of course, Laura May knew that. If she had any sense, she'd virtually drag her mother out of this city as quickly as possible. But somehow, she couldn't face the thought of her mother's retreat from sanity. Having gone through it more than once under the most trying of conditions, she lacked the strength to do so again.

The clattering sounds of overloaded wagons and the frantic cries of a great multitude of people attempting to flee the threatened city came to them clearly through the closed windows. All of Columbia was in turmoil. The railway station could no longer hold the hysterical crowds pleading for evacuation. Having declared martial law, the authorities could do nothing more than try to stem the worst of the panic.

Most frightening of all was the acrid smell of burned cotton that permeated the air. It seemed especially strong on Cousin Maude's block, for someone had put a torch to the great heap of bales stacked ten high in one of the empty lots. A volunteer fire company had managed to extinguish the flames before they spread to the nearby buildings, but it had been too close a call. It took very little imagination to know what was going to happen when Sherman's army came rampaging through the streets.

The past few weeks had been almost unbearable for Laura May. All kinds of speculations and rumors had circulated through the city. Everyone knew that Sherman was on the march again, but there was uncertainty as to where he was going. Some said Augusta, others, Branchville. Most felt certain that it would be Charleston. Very few believed it would be Columbia.

Columbia was considered a safe city. People had swarmed here from all over the South—from Louisiana, Georgia, Tennessee, and even Virginia. Charleston's bankers and merchants were so certain it would be their city that would take the brunt of the attack that they had transferred most of their wealth to the upcountry capital. Where once there had been only four banks in Columbia, now there were fifteen. Columbia was the depository for the Confederacy's mint. Wealthy planters from all over the South had sent their most prized possessions here for safekeeping. It was unimaginable that Sherman would actually attack this city when places like Augusta and Charleston could be his for the taking.

But the unthinkable *was* happening. Cousin Maude's dire predictions were coming true. "They're a pack of fools, these politicians and military men!" she'd said. "They've miscalculated this war from the very beginning. And the danger they've put Columbia in is nothing short of criminal! Why, just look at all of the cotton they've brought in here—tinder dry and ready to explode with the first spark that touches it! And the whole place is awash with whiskey. If there were ever a more dangerous combination than that, I certainly haven't heard of it!"

Others had said the same things, but no one had listened to them. Hard liquor, especially whiskey, was almost as plentiful in Columbia as water. The city had its own breweries, but with the onset of hostilities, thousands of kegs and barrels had also been shipped here from the rest of the South for safe storage. Most of these vast supplies were kept tightly locked up in warehouses and storage basements. Sadly, very few of Columbia's leading citizens had stopped to consider what might happen if their crowded city should suddenly find itself overwhelmed by an invading army thirsty for liquor.

Laura May thought of this now as she watched her mother's troubled face. What date was this? she wondered. In all of the turmoil, she had lost track of the days. Was it February 15th? Yes, of course. Yesterday had been Valentine's Day. In an effort to cheer her mother, she had decorated a red paper heart that she'd found in a drawer. It hadn't been very fancy—some scraps of lace, a few pieces of an old doily, anything to take Mama's mind off their troubles.

"Mama, I have an idea," she said now as she turned once again to face her mother. It was disconcerting to see the glassy look in those strained eyes. "Why don't you and I go upstairs together? We'll do just as you say, Mama. We'll wait until the morning. Perhaps the roads will have cleared some by then. I'll just pack a few of our things tonight so they'll be handy if we should need them."

Laura May could see Maude's disapproving expression, but she ignored it. Compromise had worked with Mama before; perhaps it would do so again.

Marian gave her daughter a weak smile. "You're such a good child, Laura May. Wait until I tell your papa how understanding you've been. He'll be so proud of you!"

"Yes, Mama." Laura May could feel the prickle of tears at the corner of her eyes. She might just as well pretend that Papa was still alive. What did it matter now? False or not, pretense was the only thing that gave Mama any real peace of mind.

Leaving Cousin Maude standing in the parlor, valise in hand, Laura May and her mother ascended the narrow staircase that led to the upstairs bedrooms. A window had been left ajar in the hallway. The draft of cold air that came through the opening had the smell of rain in it. The wind was picking up. Branches rattled against the sides of the house. A loose shutter began to creak ominously. It would be a bad night for traveling. It would be a bad night to have to wander along the road as a homeless refugee.

After tucking her mother into bed, Laura May pulled an old wooden rocking chair close to the window so she could keep watch on the street below. There would be no thought of sleep now. If there was to be a full-scale invasion, the noise of it would be far too deafening for sleep. But it wasn't an invasion that Laura May most feared. With the citizens of Columbia deserting the city in droves, the more lawless elements would now have free rein to loot and plunder at will. These were the ones whom she feared the most. If at all possible, she must keep her mother safe from such men during the long, dark hours of this night.

Suddenly startled by a creaking noise in the hallway, Laura May turned to see Cousin Maude standing in the doorway. The elderly woman's face was drawn tight with strain. A stray lock of gray hair had slipped loose from the tight bun that sat at the nape of Maude's neck. She had taken her hat off, and now she held it clutched in her trembling hands.

"I can't leave you alone, girl," she said in a whisper. "Not with your mother in this state. It wouldn't be Christian of me."

Laura May gave Maude a weak smile. "Thank you," she said simply. She felt too tired to say more.

Despite all of her good intentions to stay awake and alert, during that long evening, Laura May drifted off to sleep. What first awakened her was a dream. At least she thought it was a dream. She was in her own bed at home on Coosaw—no, it wasn't her room, it was Mama and Papa's room. In the distance, there was a terrible thundering noise. She could feel the floor shaking. Mama was sitting at the foot of the bed with Papa's long Carolina musket lying across her knees. Suddenly, there was a brilliant flash of light and a noise so deafening that Laura May sat bolt upright and let out a scream.

To her dismay, she found that she hadn't dreamt the noise at all. Nor had she dreamt the bright flash of light or her own wild scream. Mama was standing next to her, but there was no musket in her hands. And the floor *was* rattling. The whole house was rattling!

The invasion! It had come while she had slept. What a fool

she had been for not insisting with Cousin Maude that they leave that night!

"MAMA! GET AWAY FROM THE WINDOW!"

Laura May plunged at her mother, pushing her back toward the bed. *"GET UNDER THE BED, MAMA! HURRY!"*

This was much worse than what they had gone through during the battle of Port Royal Sound. They had been miles away from the fighting then. Now they were right in the middle of it.

A tidal wave of repercussive explosions came at them. The sounds of screaming were everywhere. Almost suffocated by the thick pall of smoke that seeped through every crack and cranny, Laura May found herself gasping for breath.

"Oh, dear God, don't let us die!" She pressed herself to the floor and put her arms over her head. She could hear her mother sobbing beside her and someone else, perhaps Maude, praying out loud.

It seemed like hours before the worst of the bombardment finally ceased. Stunned beyond her ability to respond, Laura May could only lie there on the floor while her whole body trembled in terror. Mama's sobbing had ceased, but she, too, was trembling with fear.

"Laura May? Marian? Are you all right?" It was Cousin Maude. Her voice sounded very distant.

Turning slightly so that she could look out into the hallway, Laura May was shocked to find that Maude was actually lying very close to her. She reached up and rubbed gently at her ears. The violent shelling must have damaged her hearing.

"I—I think that it's stopped," said Maude. "Perhaps—for the time being, at least—we're safe."

Laura May couldn't answer. She couldn't even turn to see if her mother was still beside her. There was a terrible cramped feeling in her legs, and her feet and hands had gone all numb.

"I'm going to try to get downstairs to make sure that the doors and windows are securely locked," Maude said as she pushed herself slowly up onto her feet. "Stay here, Laura May. If you can, help your mother up onto the bed."

Somehow, Laura May managed to extricate both herself and

her mother from under the bed. Mama was still shaking violently and mumbling some unintelligible phrase over and over again.

"It's all right, Mama. I'm here. I'm right here beside you. Everything will be fine now. Cousin Maude has gone downstairs to check the locks on the doors."

The frightening morning stretched slowly out. Beyond the locked doors, they could hear the tread of marching feet. Commands were being shouted back and forth as the soldiers of Sherman's army set about occupying the city. By midafternoon, a strained peace seemed to have settled over the city. Perhaps all would be well after all. Perhaps Columbia would fare every bit as well as Savannah had.

Not daring to go outside to see what was really happening, the three women huddled together in the upstairs bedroom. Not even Maude had the courage to venture another trip downstairs, though by late afternoon they were all suffering from both thirst and hunger.

The boisterous laughing and swearing of drunken men were the first indications that their troubles were about to begin all over again. The afternoon was slowly fading into a shadowy evening. After subsiding only slightly during the day, the wind started picking up again. And in the air was the ominous smell of burning cotton.

From somewhere outside, Laura May heard the unmistakable sound of splintering wood, followed by a triumphant shout. Filled with the heady exhilaration of victory, a roaming band of soldiers had found a storage house overflowing with whiskey barrels. In minutes, the street was filled with carousing men, most of them drunk or nearly so.

Plucking up her courage, Laura May crept close to the window. What she saw in the street below made her heart almost climb into her throat. A boisterous crowd of shouting, stumbling soldiers careened back and forth from one house to the other. They shot randomly into the windows, slicing at the fences with the sharp edges of their bayonets and kicking in gates and doorways as they came. Several men carried lighted torches.

As Laura May watched in horror, one of the torch bearers stumbled toward the great pile of cotton bales that had only the day before been saved from burning. The man somehow managed to climb to the very top of the heap, the torch still clutched in his hand. There was a crescendo of curses and shouts as the drunkards below urged the man on top of the bales to extinguish his torch.

It was too late. Lifting his fist aloft, the soldier shouted one last obscenity, then plunged down toward the ground, dragging the torch behind him. At first, it was only the dried burlap covering the bales that sparked up and began to burn. Long tongues of flame licked their way skyward. And then, with one blinding explosion, the whole pile of cotton went up in flames. The luckless soldiers who were too drunk to get away were literally engulfed in fire.

Stumbling backward, pressing her hands to her ears to shut out the terrible agony of the screaming men, Laura May felt her legs collapse beneath her. But the terror of what was happening outside would not release her. Crawling back toward the window, she could see that the night-darkened sky was gradually turning to a reddish orange. Small bits of cotton, looking for all the world like snowflakes, began drifting past the window. When they reached the level of the roof, they were caught by the growing wind. And now there was a virtual blizzard of cotton. Sparks from the fire whipped upward and caught at the blowing flakes. Suddenly, the snowstorm was a firestorm!

It took only minutes for the nearby trees to catch fire. Clouds of sparks and burning cotton swirled through the air. They fell onto the roofs of the houses lining the street. Tongues of flame licked hungrily at the eaves and then at the wooden siding. Stupefied and literally transfixed by the sight she was witnessing, Laura May stood rooted to the spot. The destructive power of the fire was mesmerizing. She could hear Cousin Maude shouting something from the doorway, but she was helpless to respond.

"Laura May! Laura May! Dear God, the whole place is going up! Hurry, we've got to get out of here!"

Still she stood by the window, wanting desperately to move, but somehow unable to do so. And then, suddenly, she was aware of a new activity in the street below. Coming through the flames was a large wagon. It was moving erratically, as though the fire itself were drawing it. But then she noticed a man standing in the driver's seat, a whip flashing over his head as he urged the wild-eyed mule forward. The animal reared in terror, plunged ahead, then reared again.

A black man ran alongside the wagon. He had his hands over his head to protect his face from the searing heat, but he was obviously searching for something. When the wagon was almost abreast of Cousin Maude's house, the black man suddenly stopped and began pointing upward. She could see from his face that he was shouting something to the driver.

The wagon came to a sudden halt. Throwing the reins to the black man standing on the street, the driver leapt down and came running toward the front steps. He was tall and lanky, but Laura May saw nothing familiar about him.

Within seconds, there was a frantic pounding on the front door. Laura May turned toward the hallway, but for some reason, her legs felt like they wouldn't support her. It was as though some invisible force had suddenly left her weak and unable to move.

Someone was shouting her name. "Laura May! Laura May, are you in there?" The voice was oddly familiar.

"Hello? Is anyone in there? Answer me!"

The sounds of splintering wood reverberated through the house. Still engulfed in this haze that kept her almost paralyzed with fear, Laura May was only dimly aware that the driver of the wagon was trying to kick the front door in. And then there were sounds of booted feet running up the stairway.

The bedroom door crashed against the wall with such force that it broke loose from its hinges. Cousin Maude let out a shout, then leapt forward, grasping wildly at the man who stood in the doorway. "Thank God!" she cried. "You've come to save us!"

Everything seemed to happen in slow motion. The tall, lanky figure moved forward as he pushed Maude gently aside. He reached out his arms and pulled Laura May toward him. She could feel the rapid pounding of his heart against the wall of his chest. His clothes smelled of burned ashes, and his hands were hot against her face.

"I found you," he whispered into her ear. "Oh, thank God, I've found you!"

Looking up into the soot-blackened face that hovered over hers, Laura May suddenly realized what was happening. "Jonathan?" she asked, her voice barely audible. "Is—is it really you? B-but where—how—how did you find me?"

She could feel Jonathan's muscles grow suddenly taut. "There's no time!" he shouted as he looked over his shoulder toward the window, which was now outlined by bright orange flames. "We've got to get out of this house immediately!" As he talked, he began pulling Laura May toward the doorway. Then he reached out and grasped Cousin Maude by the arm. "You go down first," he shouted. "And watch the stairs. They're already burning."

"No! Wait, Jonathan!" Laura May pulled away from him and ran back into the bedroom. "Mama's still here! We must get Mama!"

The room was fast filling with a choking pall of smoke. Laura May rushed to the bed and pulled at her mother's shoulders, trying desperately to lift her. "Mama! Mama! Please get up. We've got to get away from here as quickly as possible!"

Nothing happened. Mama lay there as still as the grave. Laura May felt a hand tugging at her arm. "It's too late, child." Cousin Maude was standing beside her. "Your mother's dead, Laura May. It was her heart, I think. She just couldn't take any more. Leave her now. She's found peace at last."

The room around her faded away into darkness as Laura May slumped forward onto her mother's body. Sweeping her up in his arms, Jonathan rushed down the stairs, followed closely by Cousin Maude. They had barely gotten off the front porch when the entire house exploded in flames. A great wall of fire, driven skyward by the powerful force of the wind, reared up behind them.

Terrified, the mule reared up, then kicked frantically at its traces. Struggling against the jolting movements of the wagon, Jonathan and the elderly black man managed to lift Laura May and then Maude into the canvas-covered buckboard. Several tongues of flame were already eating at the smoke-blackened fabric, but the old man beat them out with a blanket. Ripping off his jacket, Jonathan threw it over the mule's head. Then he grasped the trailing reins and began leading the frightened animal forward.

Nothing less than the grace of God and a sheer determination to survive got them through the inferno of that blazing city. As the early-morning sun rose into a sky seared and blackened by the terrible events of the previous night, the exhausted party of refugees found themselves standing on a small hill overlooking what was left of Columbia. Laura May felt that she had no more tears left to shed. The city lay in smoldering ruins behind them. Only a few blackened walls and broken chimneys remained. Wisps of smoke still ascended upward from the burned timbers and overheated bricks.

Dazed by the magnitude of their loss, Columbia's remaining citizens were already sifting through the rubble, searching for small mementos that through some strange miracle might have been left untouched. An elderly woman, her head in her hands, was sitting in the blackened remains of a chair. A scruffy-looking dog, the fur on his back badly singed, was sniffing around a sludge-filled crater that had once been the basement of a home. And Mama was gone. It was impossible to identify even the street where Maude's comfortable little house had once stood. The stores, the factories, the government buildings—they had all disappeared in the terrible conflagration. And who was at fault? General Sherman? His drunken soldiers? The embittered Union captives released from Columbia's cruel prison camp? The people of Columbia themselves? It didn't really matter now. It was over.

"Where shall we go, Jonathan?" It was the first words that Laura May had spoken since they had managed their daring escape. Too exhausted to answer, Jonathan could only shrug his shoulders. He felt bone weary. The pain in his burned hands was excruciating. Thus far, he had kept his agony from Laura May, but it took everything he had just to remain standing on his feet.

Maude brushed the soot from her torn dress and stepped forward. "Are you going to stay with your Mister Sherman?" she asked, the sarcasm in her voice only slightly hidden by the thankfulness she felt for what Jonathan had done for them.

"No," answered Jonathan wearily. "I'm finished with General Sherman's army."

"You're going to desert, then?" Maude asked.

"Desert? No, ma'am, I wouldn't call it that. I'm just going to let them go on without me." Jonathan let out a tired sigh. "I won't be missed—not in the least. I'm not their kind of soldier, you see."

"Hmpf," answered Maude, "I'm right thankful for that!" Without another word, she turned on her heels and walked back toward the wagon.

"We'll go to Charleston," Laura May said quietly.

"Charleston?" Jonathan turned to look at her. "Why Charleston?"

With her eyes slowly filling with tears that she thought she could no longer shed, Laura May bowed her head. "Because," she said, "it's the only place we've got left to go to."

Chapter 13

At Home and Free!
(1866)

More than a year had gone by since the destruction of Columbia, and now Laura May was traveling the road from Charleston to Beaufort which led through piney woodlands smelling of decayed leaves and rich, moist soil. Occasionally, like the swift passage of a swooping gull, the wind would weave in the tangy smell of the sea. Though unseen, the sea was a presence that was always felt. And to Laura May Weldon, it was a presence that brought back the vivid memories of a golden childhood.

The war was over at last. Still reeling from her losses, the South was busy sifting through the remains: plucking out the living, searching for the lost, burying the dead. So many gone. So many unaccounted for. And for refugees like Laura May, there weren't even families to go home to. The world had changed drastically since those distant days when gracious manners shrouded the destructive powers that had fostered human slavery.

Laura May sat rigidly in the open oxcart as it jolted its way over the corduroy roadbed. In days gone by, Papa would never have allowed her to be subjected to such primitive transportation. She would have ridden in comfort on a cushioned train seat. Or better yet, she would have traveled first class in a fast sloop as it plied its way from one coastal city to the next. But

144

Papa was gone. And the tracks that had once covered this route had mostly been destroyed—ripped up by Sherman's bummers and twisted into the shape of bow ties. The sloops were still out there, of course, but they were not for the likes of her. Now they carried only Northern speculators, who, having grown rich on the profits of war, were eagerly heading south to grab up the confiscated lands and the former homesites of the defeated.

Laura May wasn't bitter about this. She had survived, and that was enough. But she was terribly homesick. Coosaw Island lay out there in that shimmering mist, which miragelike, constantly altered the appearance of the distant horizon. The island called to her as clearly as the voices in her head that told her that despite the war, this marshy landscape would always be a part of her. And now *she* was going home.

Letting her eyes drop to her lap, Laura May gazed intently at the little packet of envelopes that lay there. One of the letters, the very topmost, was from Jonathan. It had been postmarked in the Northern city of Philadelphia, but Laura May knew that it had originated in Maryland. Jonathan had written it while sitting in the library at Johns Hopkins University. What's more, she had no need now to even open the envelope to know the contents of the letter, for she'd memorized it days ago:

My Dearest Laura May,

How dreadfully I miss you, and how I long to once again see your sweet, smiling face! Thank God, this difficult semester is nearly over! Then there will be just two more years, and I'll have my medical degree. Naturally I must pass all of my exams, but of that, I am quite confident, for I have applied myself well. Father has asked me to join him in his practice in Philadelphia when I'm through. I have already told him that such a course would be quite impossible. He seemed rather upset at first, but I think, when he meets you, he will be most understanding. It is imperative that

Father accepts the idea that I fully intend to open my own practice in Beaufort.

Will you wait that long, my darling girl? Will you wait for me to do what I know must be done if we are to succeed in our life together?

With all my love,

Jonathan

Laura May couldn't help but smile to herself as she thought of Jonathan's pleading questions. Would she wait for him? How could she do otherwise! He was the dearest thing in her life now. She couldn't even imagine living without him. But, oh yes, the waiting would be terribly hard.

Still, she had enough to occupy her time for the present. There was the teacher's training course at Charleston's Home for Confederate Widows and Orphans. The enclosed grounds of that lovely place in the very heart of the coastal city had become almost sacred to her, for it was there that she had at last found peace.

How well she remembered the day when Jonathan had left her there. After what she had gone through in Columbia—the invasion of Sherman's army, the inferno that had destroyed the city, the fearful loss of her mother—how unfair it seemed that she now be parted from Jonathan too. They had desperately wanted to stay together, but of course, with the war still on, that was quite impossible.

She'd be finished with her training course in less than a year, but she still had so much to learn about teaching. What she really needed was some practical experience. How she had prayed that an opportunity would open up for her in Beaufort! And now, thanks to Angel's contacts with the missionary school on St. Helena Island, her prayers had been answered.

Thinking of this longed-for opportunity, Laura May sifted through the little stack of letters. Here was the one from Miss Laura Towne inviting her to come to the Penn Center School for a visit. And here was the formal, but most-welcomed, letter from the superintendent of schools in Beaufort offering her a teaching position. The pay for a first-year teacher would be dreadfully meager, but Laura May was determined that she'd get by. And with luck, perhaps she could even spend her weekends on Coosaw. She'd have to stay with Angel and Maum Beezie, if they'd have her. And, of course, she knew they would.

Can you just imagine it! Laura May chuckled under her breath. The daughter of the planter who had once owned Coosaw, staying in a cabin that he had built to house his slaves. *Ah yes*, she thought, *times certainly have changed!*

But it would be a privilege to stay in that snug little cabin. And it would give her the greatest of joy just to walk across the grounds of the lovely plantation house that she had once called home. She knew she would have to come face to face with the ghosts of many old memories, but thankfully, none of them frightened her now. Laura May had long since come to terms with her past.

Finally, there would be that most happy of all events—a plantation wedding. Not just any wedding, though. No, this one was to be very special, for at long last, Angel had agreed to marry Samuel. The happy couple were to "jump de broomstick," as the Gullah folk called it, in just one week's time. This was why she was going back to Coosaw before her own school term ended.

Rumbling uncomfortably along in the slow-moving oxcart, Laura May had only one real concern. She knew nothing of the whereabouts of her brother Gilly. The last time she had heard from him, he had been living in Savannah. Then Sherman had taken the city. The invasion, when compared to what had happened in Atlanta and Columbia, had been more or less peaceful, but there was no telling what might have become of the city's routed defenders.

Likewise, Gilly probably had no way of knowing what had become of her. And most certainly he didn't know of Mama's death. Time and again, Laura May had thought of writing to the military authorities occupying Savannah to see if they could locate

Gilly, but each time she had thought better of it. What if Gilly had chosen not to sign the loyalty oath? What if he was still in hiding? What if he was dead? The thought of going through one more loss was almost more than she could bear.

Trying to push thoughts of Gilly to the back of her mind, Laura May concentrated instead on the beauty of the landscape. The wide-open vistas of marsh and sky, the rolling waves that rippled across the fields of greening spartina grass. Spring was coming to the Low Country, and the air was once more filled with the soft magic of the southern trade winds. It was just how she had always remembered it.

The roadway reached a tiny hamlet, then turned sharply to the east. Now the terrain was becoming even more familiar. The land was slightly higher here, covered liberally with pines and hardwoods. Gradually, the woodlands gave way to newly plowed fields—not cotton, as in the old days—but staples like corn and collard greens. Ramshackle houses and dilapidated barns sprouted from the earth like so many wind-torn mushrooms. Little black children were everywhere, all of them barefoot, and wearing—if anything—the most tattered of clothes.

As they approached the town of Beaufort, the buildings took on a more substantial look. Many of them sported fresh coats of paint and newly coppered roofs. The military presence was still very much in evidence. Officers wearing Union blue and soldiers of all descriptions sauntered along the streets as though they had always been a part of this town.

The cart rounded a curve, and Laura May let out a gasp. There, in an area that had once held a grassy field surrounded by stately groves of live oaks, lay a cemetery, the dimensions of which she had never seen before. Line upon line of new white headstones stretched out into the distance. This, then, she realized, was Beaufort's testament to the war. The city had become a place destined to care for, and in most cases, bury, those who had fought in the terrible battles that had almost destroyed the nation.

It was only when they reached the Whitehall Ferry that would take them across the river to Ladies Island that Laura

May could once more compose herself. But now that she was within a few miles of Coosaw, she began to feel nervous. How many of those who had been left behind would she recognize? How much would they have changed? Angel would be a grown woman now. And Maum Beezie, who had already been old when Laura May left—well—she must be truly ancient by now. Gullah Jim was gone. Zach was gone. But Samuel was still there, thankfully. Would she recognize him? More to the point, would any of them recognize her?

Laura May looked down ruefully at her faded dress. Donated by one of the benevolent women of Charleston, it had become more misshapen and sacklike with each washing. And her hair—that was a total disaster! Once lustrous and full of golden highlights, now it hung close to her head in listless clumps that bore no resemblance to its former glory.

Worst of all, Laura May knew that she was pitifully thin. The food at the Confederate Home was adequate but hardly nutritious. How often her stomach had rebelled at having to digest the mushy meal and the weevily grits! But she had no right to complain when she was being cared for by those who barely had enough for themselves. She had a roof over her head and a bed to sleep in. And she was getting a good education that would prepare her to support herself. That was a lot to be thankful for.

Pulling a broken bit of mirror out of an old reticula that she had been given, Laura May inspected her bonnet. Like her dress, it was sadly out of fashion, something from the late 1850s. Sighing, Laura May put the mirror back into her reticula. Her looks would have to do; there was no way of fixing them.

The oxcart covered the last few miles to Coosaw with an exasperating slowness. The air was filled with the sweet smell of honeysuckle, but Laura May was too nervous to notice it. And then, suddenly, they were there. Before them lay Lucy Point Creek, its coffee brown waters moving swiftly as they were sucked into the wide Coosaw River by the outgoing tide. *How strange*, thought Laura May. *This creek used to look so terribly wide and forbidding when I was a child. Has it shrunk, or is it my memories that are shriveling?*

She sat in the cart and waited as the flatbed boat used for a ferry was poled across the water to the northwestern embankment. A muscular black man whom she did not recognize was manning the ferry. He nodded deferentially to her, and she nodded back.

If Laura May had expected a welcoming committee at the ferry, she would have been sadly disappointed. But as she had sent only the briefest of messages to say that she would be arriving sometime within the week, she had no unrealistic expectations. One could never be certain about arrivals when the distance to be covered must be done in an oxcart.

Still, she felt a surge of joy as the familiarity of the island surrounded her. It was like walking into a well-loved room and finding the furniture rearranged, but comfortably so. The cart lumbered through the soft sand that covered the roadway. Butterflies flitted across open fields covered with spring flowers. The smell of wild plum blossoms filled the air with a succulent fragrance. And then, ahead of her, was the long avenue flanked by rows of great, moss-covered oaks. The same oaks she had run under, the same branches she had climbed on in those distant days of childhood!

And then, just as suddenly, the trees opened up, and Weldon Oaks lay before her. Home! The solid old house still stood, its wide lawns sloping gracefully down to the sparkling waters of the Coosaw River. There was the window of what had been her very own bedroom. And there was the piazza where she had studied her lessons on hot summer days. The cassena bushes where Angel had lost her slate and crutches were still growing profusely around the front of the house. The herb garden where they had spent so many happy hours was gone, having been replaced by what appeared to be a patch of brambles. But over in the corner of the yard, Mama's rose garden was still recognizable.

Swamped by a sudden surge of memories, Laura May felt that she would be overcome by the desire to run up the front steps of the house and call out for her family.

"Mama, are you upstairs? It's me, Laura May. I've come home, Mama! I've come back, just as I promised I would!"

"Papa, is that you in the study? Oh, how good it is to see you again!"

"Gilly? Zach? Where are you? Can't I please go down to the river and go fishing with you?"

The ghostly memories vanished. The house was occupied, but not by anyone she knew. No one came out to greet her. The wide front door remained firmly closed. No familiar, welcoming faces peered out of the windows.

The sound of a hesitant footfall made her suddenly alert. Then, tentatively, someone spoke her name.

"Laura May?"

Spinning around, Laura May found herself face to face with a young black woman whom, despite having to support herself with a single crutch, stood very tall and straight. Her coal black hair had such a sheen to it that it almost reflected the sunlight. The wide-set eyes were bright and filled with happiness. A gentle smile played about the softness of her lips.

"Angel? Is it you?"

The dark eyes filled with tears of happiness. Dropping her crutch, Angel reached out to her long-lost friend. They fell into each other's arms, weeping, hugging, unable to talk because of the depth of their emotions.

Samuel stood in the background, his face wreathed in smiles. Finally, when he could stand the waiting no longer, he stepped forward and touched Laura May's shoulders. "Dere's somebody else what's waitin' ta see you, gal, an' dere hain't no point in makin' she wait no longer."

The three of them walked together down the familiar wooded path that led to the little cabin beneath the pines. The old wooden door, weathered to a soft gray by so many years of sunshine and rain, creaked open on its worn leather hinges.

The elderly woman who sat in a high-backed wheelchair just inside the doorway looked so wizened and bent that Laura May could not stop herself from gasping out loud. But then the wrinkled old eyes began to twinkle. A small hand, twisted and birdlike, reached out toward Laura May.

"Honey lamb, es dat you?"

"Yes, Maum Beezie! Oh yes, it's me, Laura May. And I've come home to you, Maum Beezie! I've come home!"

Maum Beezie pushed herself up in her chair. "I done heard dat you es comin' back ta Bo'fort fo' ta be a teacher. Es dat de trut', chil'?"

"Yessum, it's true." Laura May fell easily into the talk of her childhood. "And Angel, she's a full-fledged nurse and midwife now, isn't she? You must be so proud of her!"

Maum Beezie's eyes fairly glowed as she nodded in response. "Hain't I done always said dat you two chilluns was gwanna turn inta sumpin' special!"

Feeling pleased but slightly embarrassed, Laura May could only nod. "I've come back for Angel's wedding, Maum Beezie. It thrilled me so to hear that she and Samuel were going to get married. The trip was a bit hard, but wild horses couldn't have kept me from coming for such a wonderful event!"

Maum Beezie's face crinkled up into a toothless grin. "Dey hain't de onliest ones dat's gwanna jump de broomstick, honey lamb."

"Oh?" Laura May was genuinely surprised. Who else was going to get married besides Samuel and Angel? Her mind raced through a list of the various youngsters who had lived in the quarters before she had left Coosaw, but no other possibilities came to mind.

There was an amused twinkle in Maum Beezie's eyes now. Angel moved closer to Laura May. She placed her arm around her friend's shoulders and drew her close. "We got de bes' surprise fo' you, Laura May. Like Maum Beezie says, dere's gwanna be two weddin's at Coosaw, an' dat's why et's so impo'tant dat you had ta come home."

"Who?" asked Laura May, her voice filled with perplexity. "Who else is going to be married besides you and Samuel?"

Angel reached out and grasped both of Laura May's hands. "Et's yo bruddah." Her answer was spoken gently but with great feeling. "You own bruddah, Gilly, an' his sweet li'l gal from

Sabannah. Dey's gwanna get hey'e jes as soon as dey kin. Den we all fo'—she glanced lovingly back toward Samuel—"Sam'l an' me an' Gilly wid his gal, we es all gwanna jump de broomstick tugedda."

Laura May stood in the center of the floor, feeling that the earth itself was beginning to tilt recklessly beneath her feet. "Gilly? You've found him? He's coming here to Coosaw?"

"Yes, Lawd, an' praise 'E name!" answered Maum Beezie, her voice suddenly taking on a newfound strength. "De Lawd, 'E gibs, an' de Lawd, 'E takes away, but et's de giben' dat weuns has gotsta 'members de most. All de pain what comes from de takin' way, well-suh, child, dat soon's gwanna pass on." She closed her eyes and raised her face toward the ceiling.

There was a strange silence in the room as Maum Beezie gathered her thoughts. Then she began to hum an old spiritual. It was such a familiar sound to Laura May that she felt her head begin to slowly nod up and down in time with the rhythm.

The words came out slowly, for Maum Beezie's voice was frail and trembling:

> De ol' sheep done kno' de road.
> De ol' sheep done kno' de road.
> De ol' sheep done kno' de road.
> De young lam' mus' find de way.

Then Samuel's strong bass voice took up the words:

> Shout, my bruddah, you are free!
> De young lam' mus' find de way.
> Christ has brought yo' liberty!
> De young lam' mus' find de way.

Maum Beezie rubbed her arthritic knees and began to smile knowingly. "An dat's what's gwanna carry dis ol' 'omans straight t'rough inta Glory Land, chilluns!" she said, her voice almost triumphant.

Laura May flung her arms around the elderly woman. "Oh, thank you, Maum Beezie!" she said earnestly. "Thank you for all of the times you believed in me. It was your faith that pulled me through, you know." Leaning forward, she kissed first one wrinkled cheek and then the other.

"No, chil'," she said quietly. "Et was yo' own faith what pulled you t'rough." Then, almost as an afterthought, she added, "Dough I do 'spect dat mah prayin' had a might bit ta do wid et."

Looking up toward the ceiling once more, the elderly woman's eyes filled with tears. "T'anks You, Lawd," she said. "Mah young lambs, dey's sho nuff hab found dey way, jes' like You promise me dey would!" Then she bowed her head and hummed quietly into her hands while above her little cabin, the gentle winds of the South Carolina Sea Islands sang their old, old song as they brushed through the branches of the tall loblolly pines.

Epilogue

Exiting busy Interstate 95 onto South Carolina's State Highway 21, you head east toward the city of Beaufort. For the discerning traveler, this can be a passage back into time. As you approach the area known as the "Low Country," open vistas of shining rivers and golden marshes connected by a hundred tiny creek beds come into view. Ignoring the strip shopping centers, convenience stores, and multitude of motels can be challenging, but the past is there, lurking behind all of these brash attempts at modernization.

Beaufort itself provides a glance backward into the gentility of the antebellum era. Thanks to the Union's early conquest of the city and its citizens' long-standing sense of historical significance, much of Beaufort's architectural finery has been preserved. The military cemetery is there lining the north side of Highway 21, with row upon row of white headstones, sad remembrances to the follies of war. The fine homes where families like the imaginary Weldons lived in very unfictitious opulence still dominate the waterfront. And if you are observant, you may still see tree-lined tracks leading to old plantation homes.

Beaufort's open-armed salute to what "once was" now readily takes in all of its history with a knowing shrug. Tourists are a common sight on Bay Street. Southerners and Northerners alike, blacks and whites, the affluent and the commoner—all are accepted for their mere presence rather than their past ancestry.

It was, however, not always this way. Some of the historic landmarks are just recently being recognized for the contributions they played in this nation's well-meaning, though often ill-starred, attempts at equality. One such place is Penn Center on St. Helena Island, the school for freed slaves that was founded by the Union missionaries during the earliest stages of the Civil War.

It was here, at Penn Center, where I first got my inspiration to write the Weldon Oaks Series. One day, while standing in the old cemetery that lies on a gentle knoll of land just to the south of the Brick Church* where Laura Towne conducted her very first classes for the freedmen, I was struck by the overwhelming selflessness of the deeds done here. Walking through the magnificent grove of ancient live oaks that had been witness to so many momentous events, I came across Penn Center's museum, a building housing a collection of artifacts including old photographs, documents, and diaries. It was here that I began to visualize the characters who would inhabit my stories.

Virtually all of the historic people and events portrayed in the Weldon Oaks Series are as close to being factual as I am capable of making them. Laura Towne was a real woman and a untiring missionary. She lived out her life on the South Carolina Sea Islands, giving all of her energies to the people she had come to serve. Miss Towne died on St. Helena Island in the year 1901. A beautiful monument to her dedicated work may be found in the cemetery near Penn Center's Old Brick Church.

Traveling just a few miles farther down the road from Penn Center, one comes to the gutted and crumbling remains of the Chapel of Ease. It was here, on that fateful November morning of 1861, that the parishioners of St. Helena first learned of the approach of the armada of Yankee warships bearing down upon them.

Coosaw Island is also very real, though to the best of my

knowledge, no one named Weldon ever lived there. A plantation with its accompanying slave quarters did once exist on the
island. And as reported in my story, the island was heavily
picketed by Federal forces as a preventative measure against
the possible incursion of Confederate troops into the area.

My daughter and I got more than we bargained for one spring
afternoon when we decided to do some exploratory research on
Coosaw. We were walking along the island's riverbank looking
for an old slave cemetery that was reported to lie there. Sometime earlier, a shrimper, who was traveling down the river in
his boat, told of seeing what he thought was the remains of a
cypress casket being washed downriver. Becky and I managed
to find that cemetery, though not in the manner we expected
to. Pushing our way through waist-high grasses and brambles,
we ended up falling into a shallow depression—the remains of
one of the old gravesites.

During the years I spent researching and writing the Weldon
Oaks Series, I met many gracious and generous people who
were veritable fonts of information. Gerhard Spieler stands head
and shoulders atop this list. Over the years, Gerhard and his
wife, Ruth, have become truly valued friends.

Tita Heins, affectionately known to her public as Aunt Tita,
the Gullah Storyteller, gave me my first taste of the Sea Is-
landers' musical dialect. Sadly, Tita's untimely passing still
leaves me with a great feeling of loss.

Phyllis Dolislager also deserves my thanks, for she helped
me with the bulk of the research, then repeatedly proofread
and critiqued every word of all five book manuscripts. Her assistance has proved invaluable, and her close friendship is something I will always treasure.

Finally, my most heartfelt appreciation goes to my husband,
Lucien, and my daughter, Becky, for their unstinted patience
and assistance in the writing of this series. Without their encouragement, none of this work would have been possible.

I wish all my readers could take the same trip of discovery
along the highways and byways of the southeast coast's Sea
Islands that I took. The rich historical heritage to be found

there would be well worth the journey, for it teaches those who are open to listen that the freedoms we cherish today were bought with a heavy price. Nor must we ever forget that the struggle against prejudice, intolerance, and human bondage in all its forms should not cease until that glorious day when God "calls all His chilluns home!"

---

* Regular meetings continue today at the Brick Baptist Church on St. Helena Island, where the congregation still loves to sing the old spirituals, some of which have been recorded in my books. Many members of the present congregation are direct descendants of the freedmen portrayed in the Weldon Oaks Series.